A Nearer Moon

Melanie Crowder

Atheneum Books for Young Readers

New York London Toronto Sydney New Delhi

atheneum

ATHENEUM BOOKS FOR YOUNG READERS

An imprint of Simon & Schuster Children's Publishing Division

1230 Avenue of the Americas, New York, New York 10020

This book is a work of fiction. Any references to historical events, real people, or real places are used fictitiously. Other names, characters, places, and events are products of the author's imagination, and any resemblance to actual events or places or persons, living or dead, is entirely coincidental.

Text copyright © 2015 by Melanie Crowder

Cover illustration copyright © 2015 by Zdenko Basic

For information about special discounts for bulk purchases, please contact Simon & Schuster Special Sales at 1-866-506-1949 or business@simonandschuster.com.

The Simon & Schuster Speakers Bureau can bring authors to your live event. For more information or to book an event, contact the Simon & Schuster Speakers Bureau at 1-866-248-3049 or visit our website at www.simonspeakers.com.

Also available in an Atheneum Books for Young Readers hardcover edition

Cover design by Sonia Chaghatzbanian; interior design by Irene Metaxatos

The text for this book was set in Adobe Caslon Pro and Dear Sarah.

Manufactured in the United States of America

0716 OFF

First Atheneum Books for Young Readers paperback edition August 2016

10 9 8 7 6 5 4 3 2 1

The Library of Congress has cataloged the hardcover edition as follows:

Crowder, Melanie, author.

A nearer moon / Melanie Crowder. — First edition.

pages cm

Summary: Long ago the dam formed, the lively river turned into a swamp, and the wasting illness came to Luna's village, and now that her little sister is sick, Luna will do anything to save her, even offer herself to the creature that lives in the swamp on the day of the nearer moon.

ISBN 978-1-4814-4148-3 (hc)

ISBN 978-1-4814-4149-0 (pbk)

ISBN 978-1-4814-4150-6 (eBook)

1. Water spirits—Juvenile fiction. 2. Magic—Juvenile fiction. 3. Sisters—Juvenile fiction. 4. Families—Juvenile fiction. [1. Water spirits—Fiction. 2. Magic—Fiction. 3. Sisters—Fiction. 4. Family life—Fiction.] I. Title.

PZ7.C885382Ne 2015

813.6—dc23

[Fic] 2014043590

For my sisters,
Timme and Chelle

Prologue

The river flows.

It begins as a trickle deep in the heart of the jungle, in the thick, secret heart of the jungle. It surges and swirls, gorging on the breath of a thousand streams. The river, it bells, and it swells, and it flows, and a reed-thin girl on a push-pole boat skims silently by.

Just beyond a stretch that wiggles like a crimped ribbon, a log jam stops the river in its headlong sprint. Long ago the dam formed, gathering storm-tossed sticks and rising, the water creeping inch by inch to bury the silty flats, to brush the shins of trees unaccustomed to getting their feet wet. The dam rose and a swamp was born. The pent up, penned in river dove deep underground, probing through tunnels of granite and caverns of crushed rock for a place to rise again to the surface, willful and wild.

Out in the middle of the swamp, the water spirals in a lazy arc, collecting a scattering of leaf litter, a few vagabond insects, and a leisurely film of dust. A flat slick catches and holds the swill, holds still while the rest of the swamp moves in a slow waltz around it. A person who didn't know this water might think the slick was just an eddy, caught and swaddled in a crook of the swamp's arm. But the villagers, who live and breathe by the ebb and flow of the water, know to steer wide of the still spot. They know that something beneath pulls at the water, a creature that makes the water skippers tremble and the otters skitter for their dens.

Year by year, inch by inch, the villagers raised the stilts that held up their homes, until they couldn't remember anymore the sweet smell of a passing river, the eager slope of a riverbank, the sound of giggling water spilling over boulders and dancing over rocks.

The villagers marked the time in two ways: before the swamp and after. What came before was good. And all that came after was not.

1

Luna

At the edge of the swamp, rimmed round with tall marsh grasses and dotted with pulai trees dripping humid tears, a girl with long limbs and hair as dark as a moonless night stepped through the reeds and into her shallow boat.

On the hill behind her, seraya trees rustled their leaves, and a blizzard of tiny yellow flowers spun through the air. To the west, the river spilled in; to the east, the dam held back the water. In the space between, her village perched over the sweltering swamp.

Luna lifted a long steering pole and was just about to shove away from the shore when a smaller girl with the same black hair and gangly limbs called out as she ran down the hill from the garden plots.

"Take me with you!" Willow shouted.

Luna stepped one foot back on the shore to steady them both, reaching out a hand to help her little sister into the boat.

"You weren't really going without me, were you?" Willow wobbled, arms outstretched, toward the bow.

Luna chuckled. As if her little sister would ever allow that.

Willow sat cross-legged on the rough-hewn floor and rubbed the tiny pewter charm tacked to the bow for luck. She gripped the edges of the boat, her whole body twitching with excitement.

Luna tested her weight and shifted the bundle of nets at her feet. With one solid push, the flat boat drifted out of the reeds, gliding between water lilies opening to greet the late morning sun. A haze of sticky, sweaty heat hung like a cloud of gnats over the swamp.

Luna dipped her pole into the water. Hand over hand, she lowered it down until the smooth wood caught in the mud below, caught and held like a child curling her fingers into a lock of hair and gripping tight.

Luna leaned out and pulled her pole away from the reluctant mud, hand over hand. Water trickled over her knuckles, streaming down her arms and drip, drip, dripping from her elbows, until the silt-drenched tip rose into the air, dropping the mud back where it came from.

The boat wandered through a grove of waterlogged trees and under the village perched above. The huts were raised on stilts and strung together just above the waterline by walkways that swayed in the gentle winds swirling through the swamp. As they passed by, Granny Tu left her rocking chair and stepped to the railing. Her skin was wrinkled as a plum passed over by the pickers and left on the tree to wither, but her eyes were sharp and sparkling. She cupped a hand to her mouth. "Bring me back a big one."

"You bet!" Willow said.

Most of the villagers were tucked into the shadows, away from the buggy morning, but Luna's best friend, Benny, pushed back the shutters and leaned out the window of his hut to wave as they passed. His straight black hair hung like a curtain in front of his eyes, and he swept it away impatiently.

"Come over after, okay?" he called.

Luna nodded, waving in return.

She steered away from the village and between the last set of pulai trees, weaving between their buttressed roots and gliding out onto open swamp. It was quiet except for the buzzing of water bugs and the bulbuls chattering in the treetops. Quiet and empty, with only her little boat moving on top of the water.

"How was school this morning?" Luna asked.

"We did our plusses, up to a hundred. And I've got spelling lists to study tonight." Willow leaned back until she could see her sister's face, upside down and swaying as Luna pushed her pole into the mud and hefted it back out again. "You'll help me, won't you?"

Luna nodded. But Willow already knew the answer. She was the sun that the rest of them, Mama and Luna and Granny Tu, orbited around. It had always been that way. Maybe because she was so much younger than Luna, maybe because she was just a baby when Daddy died. Maybe because she was all giggles and mischief, dewy kisses and unkempt braids.

"What else?" Luna asked.

"Lily's gran brought lemon drops for snack. She told us a story of a wood sprite that lived in her rafters when she was little. They never once saw it, but if they so much as dusted the beam where its bundle-of-sticks house was, the milk would turn sour and vegetables would rot overnight." Willow shuddered with glee, slapping her hand against the rim of the boat. "No, thank you. No sprites as houseguests for me!"

"Nah, there's no such thing as sprites," Luna said. She jiggled her weight from one foot to the other, just enough to set the shallow boat rocking. Not enough to tip it over—a boat wide enough to steer through the swamp was all but impossible to tip over—but enough to set Willow squealing in giddy protest.

Luna poled to the wide mouth of the swamp where it met and slowed the steady push of the river. Just out of sight, the channel narrowed and the current picked up speed. Luna wasn't allowed past the bend in the river. Her flat-bottomed boat wasn't made for cutting through bumping, frolicking water. But some days, if she was lucky, a fish that didn't know any better would wander a little too close to the swamp and find the back of her net.

The boat slid into an eddy, and Luna cast her net out over the water. She wasn't going to catch anything, not today, with Willow's giggles startling the fish into the shadows. But on a day like this, when even the dragonflies seemed to tilt their wings to catch a little extra of the sun's sparkle, empty nets were nothing to scowl at. Willow leaned over the edge of the boat and stared down into the clear water below. Luna kept half an eye on her sister, the other half on the net she flung out and back, out and back again, just for the rhythm of it, for the feel of the rope in her hands and the coarse wood under her bare feet.

When the sun was at its highest, and it was too hot to even pretend at fishing, Luna poled away from the river and let her boat drift out into the center of the swamp. She shoved her steering pole deep into the muck, pushing faster and faster, until the boat spun, and spun, and spun, never tipping or dipping into the swamp water the tiniest bit. Willow lay on her back, gripping the edges of the boat and laughing so hard it sounded like she might choke.

"Lunaaaaaaaaa!" she shrieked.

"I'm gonna steer you straight into the slick," Luna teased.

Willow sat up and twisted to look over her shoulder at the tongue of still, filmy water at the far end of the swamp.

"That's not funny, Luna. You would not."

Luna turned the boat far away from the dead spot on the water. Of course she wouldn't, and not just because it was one of Mama's never-to-be-broken rules:

Don't go past the bend in the river.
Don't go below the dam.
Steer far away from the slick.

People said there was a creature that lived beneath the slick lying still as a gravestone on top of the water, a creature that cast a curse on the swamp and sickened anyone who drank it. But Luna didn't believe in the creature, and she didn't believe in curses.

"Of course I'm kidding," she said, setting the boat to spinning again.

Willow's laughter echoed through the swamp, and it filtered down into the layers of silty water beneath. Down through the fingers of floating weeds, down beneath the lip of an underwater cave where a wretched creature huddled and tried not to listen, tried not to hear the sound that grated most against its ears, that carved new scars into its rotten heart.

The laughter didn't stop, so the creature, no bigger than a frog, rose toward the surface. The slick moved with it. The creature rose and reached a gnarled hand toward the bobbing, spinning boat. With a tug of its tiny fingers, just a hair's breadth away from the charm tacked to the bow, it gripped the wood and dipped the boat beneath the surface, just for a second, just long enough to fill the little one's mouth, opened wide with laughter, full of black swamp water.

The laughter stopped and the boat ceased its spinning. The creature slid, unseen, back to its cave, the silence smothering its aching heart like a damp blanket over hot coals.

Willow sat up quick, her eyes wide as a startled rabbit's. Water streamed down her nose and over her temples. She sputtered and coughed the filthy swamp water off her tongue.

Luna scrambled toward her sister. "Spit it out! Spit it all out!"

Willow leaned over the side of the boat, her stomach heaving as she retched, her eyes teary and her nose running. Luna gripped her sister's slight shoulders to keep her from falling in.

When Willow leaned back at last, Luna helped her sit, wiping her lips dry with the edge of her cotton shirt. "Are you all right? I'm so sorry—we weren't anywhere near the slick—I was just teasing. I don't know what happened!"

The two girls stared in stunned silence at each other. Streaks of silt dried on Willow's face like shadows laid over a patch of sunlight. She managed a wavery grin and spat again. "Let's just go home, okay?"

Luna gripped her pole in trembling hands and settled herself at the stern on unsteady legs. She guided her boat between the pulai trees and skimmed over the swamp, never spinning or dipping or bobbing the slightest bit.

"Granny Tu will make you a pot of tea, and we'll forget this ever happened," Luna said, though the words rang false even in her ears. She knew, and Willow knew, that it was already too late.

2

Perdita

Humans have a way of possessing the land over which they walk, the water over which they travel. As they multiplied, as they staked their claim with the gnash of steam and the clash of gears, the sprites began to fade.

The woods thinned of their dancing spirits. The air seldom felt the breath of little wings stirring up the wind; the skies filled only with bugs and birds and lonely, passengerless clouds. And the water, where once the sprites had skipped like stones across the river, fey and feral, had to be content with its own splashing, and a mere handful of the tiny creatures to frolic in the frothing tips of the waves.

Perdita and Pelagia were born on the same day, in the same hour, only a few seconds of the same minute apart. All the air and wood and water sprites gathered around while they were rocked by the same wavelet, the fish below buoying them up on a pillow of bubbles. A thousand droplets leaped away from the steady flow of the river to kiss their tiny brows.

It was a rare thing for the sprites to come together, for they are fickle creatures, hardly ever enticed to hold a single thought for long. But rarer still is a birth, and the whisper of hope that comes with the newness of life. Just enough hope to believe they had a chance—if they could find another world lush with green growing things, a world where clear, clean streams flowed unfettered through the land.

Hope is uncommon but not unwelcome.

A decision was made.

Perdita and Pelagia blinked and smiled and gurgled in the contented way that newborns do, unaware of the great change they had brought, unaware of the great sorrow it would bring back upon them.

3

Luna

Home was a modest hut: a single room with a kitchen, a table cluttered with dishes or strewn with Granny Tu's charts tracking the nearing moon, and a large knotted rug spread over the bare floor. Paneled screens created two bedrooms at the back. Granny Tu and Mama shared one, and the girls shared the other. On any normal day, the hut would have been filled with the sounds of cooking or cleaning, or small feet pattering across the floorboards. On this day, however, the only sound was the uncanny stillness of held breath.

Mama, Granny Tu, and Luna stood around the edges of the bed that the girls shared, watching Willow lift spoonful after spoonful of mushroom soup to her mouth and blow to cool it.

She was sick. Not with the sniffles or a dusting of hay fever: Willow had caught the wasting sickness that arrived with the swamp, which not a single person had survived. The sickness always lasted three weeks to the day, whether the patient was young and strong or already made frail by age.

"Okay," Willow finally said, dropping her spoon. "Stop it. Granny Tu, sit down." She motioned to the worn rocking chair in the corner. "Luna, go fishing. Or go muck around with Benny. I'll be right here when you get back. Mama—"

But no one moved. Each of them looked as if she'd been struck flat across the face. Luna wanted to reach out to Mama, who stood still as a limbless snag, trunk hollow and roots rotting in the dirt below. She wanted Mama to take her hand or tuck her under her arm, to say it wasn't her fault and Willow was going to be fine.

I'm so scared, Mama.

Luna watched the side of Mama's face, willing her to turn, to look at her. But Mama didn't turn. Luna's knees wobbled and her head seemed to float atop her neck, grief pulling her loose like a boat slipping its mooring. She stumbled to the side of the bed and lifted the covers, twining her ankles around Willow's, clutching Willow's arm and pressing her cheek against her sister's shoulder, as if Willow could hold her there, could keep her from drifting away.

Willow sighed and opened her mouth for another spoonful. "Fine, then," she said. "Tell me a story."

Granny Tu moved to the rocker, gripping rails worn smooth and familiar over the years as she sank into the wide seat. She tipped the rungs back, and the wood groaned beneath her. She raised her eyes to the ceiling, searching the cobwebbed corners of her mind.

Granny Tu's tales had a way of blending together: stories that her grandmother had been told by her grandmother, of each summer when the moon drew near and the Perigee festival brought fire to the sky and cheer to the village, of the magical world hardly anyone believed in anymore, of water lizards rolling their prey into underwater caves, of Willow's first step and Luna's first word, and of the smash and bang beginning of the world. They all blended together until the truth was buried deep as the roots of the groaning pulai trees.

"Let's see," she began. "How about I tell you of the trip I have planned for you and your sister once you get better?" Granny Tu's voice trembled, and her eyes didn't lift from her swollen knuckles, clasped tight in her lap.

Willow nodded as she blew to cool her spoonful of soup.

"My poppa took your uncle Tin and me when we were about your age. We went up the turning, twisting river, up to the city that floats on a cool lake at the base of a mountain, a lake so deep and clear they say it has no bottom, no matter how far down you go. A cool, clear lake that flows under the very earth and straight out to the sea.

"There were boats driven by the wind across the water, their bright sails puffed out like the ribcages of giant beasts. Above our heads, lanterns floated like newborn clouds, rising to meet the stars burning yellow holes in the sky.

"Poppa took us through the stalls on the floating barges. They had everything you could imagine— metalworkers, falcon trainers, woodworkers, medicine makers, and every kind of sweet thing: pies, cakes, and even ice brought down from the top of the mountain and dusted with sugar and cream."

As Willow slid farther and farther down in the bed, her eyelids beginning to sag, and her breathing becoming heavy, Granny Tu's voice slowed to a murmur. Luna lifted the soup out of her sister's hands and tucked the blanket up under her chin. Granny Tu and Mama and

Luna met one another's eyes, mirrors of their own shock, their own mourning.

Willow would never go to the floating city, would never steer a boat of her own, would never see her next birthday.

Maybe Mama didn't recognize the silent plea in Luna's eyes; maybe she didn't know how the thought of losing her sister seared Luna's skin like a fever. Mama took a last look at Willow, at the rise and fall of her chest, the darting eyes under closed lids, and then she turned and walked out. Luna slid out of bed and tiptoed around the paneled screen.

"Wait!" she called out as she stepped outside.

Mama was already halfway across the walkway that led from their hut to Benny's next door. When she turned, the wooden bridge rippled beneath her.

"Mama, what can I do? Give me something to do that will make Willow better."

"There's nothing to be done," Mama said, her voice flat as a leaf driven to the ground by hard rains. "You know that."

"But we can't just sit here! We have to try—"

"You think no one has tried? You think you're the first person to lose someone?" Mama's voice broke and she clapped a hand over her mouth.

"But Granny Tu said there were medicine makers in the city. Mama, if there's a doctor, maybe he has medicine for Willow."

"Luna, I'm not going to run off to the city when Willow needs me here. There's nothing a doctor can do for her. There's nothing any of us can do." The last words were barely audible. Mama turned away and walked slowly past Benny's, past the school, and up to the chapel at the highest point in the village.

Luna folded her arms over her chest and blew an impatient breath through her nostrils. Clicking beads around and around in a circle wasn't going to do any good. Sitting by the bed and telling stories wasn't going to fix anything either.

She could be out and back in a day. Mama would be mad, but she was going to have to deal with it.

Luna was going to the lake. She was going to find that doctor.

4

Perdita

Just as air sprites skipped from one gust of wind to another and wood sprites dashed from leaf to twig to leaf again, water sprites were happiest on, or in, or near the water. Before they learned to walk, before they even learned to crawl, they were dropped into the river so they learned to swim.

To a water sprite, currents and waves were nothing to be feared. The water rose up to greet them, it swelled beneath their arms and pushed against their legs, teasing them into a paddle. Perdita and Pelagia kicked, marveling at the whorls of bubbles that spun in their wake as they swam, reveling in the silken water giving way under their hands.

Their playmates were newts and minnows; they rode on the backs of ducklings, stroking their downy feathers and tickling their little webbed feet. They played while grown-up sprites, who were strong in the air magic that lifts and carries, and the woods magic that grounds and grows, and the water magic that washes and renews, built the door that would take all of them into the next world.

The door makers began every day as the sun broke over the mountain, casting its first blush of light onto the lake below. They finished every evening as the sun ducked below the horizon again. Their nights were filled with the breathy songs of the air sprites and with the whistle of the wood sprites' flutes echoing eerily down from the heights.

If it had only been a matter of building a door from one place to another, leaving would have been a simple affair, done in a few weeks or in a few months at most. But finding the right place to go was not an easy thing. The door makers searched for a world where they wouldn't be quickly uprooted again. A place the humans had not discovered and so, defiled. A place where the waters were clear and the skies were bright and the woods were still singing as they had on the very first day.

While the door makers worked their magic, folk

circled around them. Air sprites skittered down to sniff at the mossy offerings of the wood sprites, who learned to look with a little less horror on the willful splashing of the water sprites.

The door makers worked as they searched, to be ready when the time came, and as the months passed, the door between worlds began to take shape in the air. Tall as the tallest of the sprites, and wide enough for two to pass through together side by side, it hung suspended in the air, no higher than the tips of a rabbit's ears. The door seemed to glow faintly with a light of its own, if you looked for it with the edge of your vision.

Even the humans, who bumbled and stumbled through life without any magic of their own, stepping right in the middle of a circle of stones or striding through a web of sunlight, somehow managed to avoid that space in the air, the space that seemed to hum with an energy of its own. And so the paths that wound from the humans' huts, through the jungle, and up to the garden on the hill, veered to leave the space between the two towering seraya trees alone.

"Stay close," warned Perdita and Pelagia's mother. "The door could be ready at any time."

The twins sat on either side of their mother, their backs to the door in the air, mesmerized by the light rippling on the surface of the river and the sound of water spilling over the rocks. But they did not sit still for long.

The fact that they might be leaving soon hung in the back of their minds. They had a measured number of days, an allotted number of breaths in this world, on this beautiful river that wound in curves like a ribbon through the hardwood jungle, where the humans lived in small huts set into the bare earth and long-necked waterbirds strutted in the shallows. The new world on the other side of the door might be all kinds of wonderful, might be far away from the humans, but it wouldn't be here, where the twins had first opened their eyes, where they had first greeted the water.

There was so much for them to see and for their hands, still unmarked by calluses and scars, to touch. Perdy and Gia's days were full, hunting for abandoned mollusk shells or stalking through the meadows, the tasseled tips of the grasses swaying high above their heads.

Water sprites were supposed to keep to the streams, but Perdy was never one for following rules. She skipped across the riverbank, and Gia followed after, pausing beneath the white crown of a dandelion. Perdy took hold and shook, the seeds spilling like falling leaves onto their heads and shoulders and spinning down to the dirt like upturned umbrellas. Out on the river, they sat astride the backs of young carp, tunneling through the currents and leaping over the oncoming wavelets.

Such was the bond between the twin sisters that if one lifted a hand to her chest, she would feel the echo of two hearts beating within.

Thump thump.

(Thump thump.)

Thump thump.

(Thump thump.)

Such was the bond between them that they could not be apart for long before the absence, like a living thing, took hold in the space beneath their ribs and pulsed with an aching, empty beat. But as the twins grew, each developed a nature of her own. Desires the other did not share. Pursuits the other would not follow.

For Gia, the knowledge that they would be leaving soon kept her close to her mother's side so that when the making of the door between worlds was complete and the bells tolled for all the sprites to come, she would be there. She would not be left behind.

For Perdy, that knowledge drove her farther and farther from home so that when the making of the door between worlds was complete, there wouldn't be a single cave unexplored or a single eddy undiscovered.

She was always wandering off, always getting happily lost. Always carried back home in a heron's bill or on a terrapin's back, or floating in a drifting spider's web. Every time, Gia was there to welcome her home. Every time, there were kisses and promises and tears tiny as dewdrops in Perdy's eyes.

"I'll never wander so far again," Perdy would say.

But that was a promise she could not keep.

5

Luna

It was the first of Mama's rules never to be broken: *Don't go past the bend in the river.* The swamp was all Luna knew—all she wanted to know as long as Willow, Mama, Granny Tu, and Benny were there with her. But when Willow got sick, all that changed.

So before even a hint of sunlight touched the sky, Luna tiptoed into the moonless dark. She climbed down the ladder that straddled the stilts holding their hut high above the swamp and untied her little boat from its mooring. She settled a small bundle at the bow, balanced her own weight against it, and stepped to the center of the boat's rough belly. She lifted her pole and stood, finding her legs and setting her eyes on the water before her.

The village hung over her, shadows looming, dis-approving as she poled under the walkways that stretched from hut to tree to hut like a giant fishing net flung out over the swamp. Like a net that closed in on her from above, trying to hold her there, keep her safe.

At the edge of the water, yellow eyes blinked, glow-ing faintly in the fading dark. The insects were burrowed deep in the mud and the macaques dozed in the tree-tops. The morning air wiggled with sweaty heat, waiting for the sun to rise and sizzle the moisture out of the sky. Luna shook her hair behind her and wiped her hands dry on her thin cotton shirt.

She pushed against her pole, pushed off into the middle of the swamp, away from the village. The bunch of coins in her pocket pulled at her like a weight on a fishing line. *Thief,* it bobbed. *Liar,* it tugged. Luna thrust her chin in the air. This was for Willow. Mama wouldn't care about the money if it made Willow better. And maybe Mama was so lost in her sadness anyway, so lost in the candle smoke and clicking prayer beads, that Luna could slide back home before dark, and Mama wouldn't even notice she'd been gone.

Every family in the village had lost someone to the wasting sickness, had buried resourcefulness under the heavy weight of grief. They had given up long ago on finding a cure; they had tried and failed too many times over the years to let their hopes rise, only to be dragged back down again.

But not Luna.

She had never been to the city on the lake, but the doctor Granny Tu mentioned might know how to save Willow. And Luna couldn't just sit and do nothing. She had to try.

Luna poled through the trees until at last the swamp thinned and the river began to push against her. The predawn hush of the swamp was replaced by water that shushed and leaped and splashed against the hull of her boat. The boat picked up speed, and there was no longer any space left in her mind for worrying—it all belonged to the river, to keeping the bow of her boat pointed forward and plowing through the oncoming water. If the bow ticked to either side, the current gleefully pushed against the broad side, and it was all she could do to dig in her pole and steer the boat straight again.

Even the river knew she shouldn't be out all alone before the fairy birds began their morning song and the freshwater crabs stirred in their burrows. Even the river knew such a flat boat had no business riding swift currents.

It had been her daddy's boat, and Granny Tu's before that. When Daddy died, the boat was given to Luna. Her steering pole had been no taller than she was, and the wide boat had seemed big as an island beneath her feet. She was only allowed to steer through the reeds at the edge of the swamp, with Granny Tu or Uncle Tin or sometimes Mama to bump her back into the shallows if she drifted too far.

The first time Luna had taken Willow out on the water, her sister's eyes had never stopped roving over the swamp, wondering at all the finned and fan-tailed creatures beneath. Luna bit the inside of her cheek to banish the memory that tunneled holes in her heart. Willow was going to be fine. She was.

"Hey!"

Luna's head jerked toward the riverbank, where a figure darted around the trees, waving his hands over his head and shouting.

"Your mama's gonna skin you alive!"

Luna scowled and kept poling forward, concentrating on keeping the boat pointed upriver. She shouted back over her shoulder, "If you only came out here to scold me, you should have stayed in bed!"

"Aw, come on. You know you want me along!" Benny called.

Luna ignored him, and the sound of pitter-patter footsteps along the riverbank stopped.

"I want to help Willow too, you know!"

Luna's pole snagged against a rock and the bow dipped under a curl of water that seemed to leap up out of nowhere. She lurched in the opposite direction to steady her boat as the bow speared, without so much as a nudge from her, toward the shore.

The boat slid up onto the riverbank and sliced through the reeds. Benny scrambled in, rearranging Luna's bundle behind him and shoving off, tipping until he was perched careful as a stork at the bow. He looked back and patted a lump at his side. "I brought honey cakes," he announced by way of a truce.

Luna's traitorous stomach gurgled loud enough to wake wild pigs from their slumber. Benny's shoulders shook in silent laughter, but he knew better than to let it out and give Luna even one reason to turn the boat around and dump him on the shore again.

She squinted and pushed back into the current, coaxing her boat onto the flat tongue that wove down the center of the river. The river bottom was muddy in some places and rocky in others, and if she wasn't careful, her pole would slide on a slippery stone and dump her in the water when she pushed too hard.

The sun rose while she poled in silence. With the sun came the bugs, and the fish woke with them, jumping out of the water and splashing back down all around the boat. A black-winged darter leaped out of the shadows and pumped its wings, bobbing down the pulsing vein of the river, leading the way before them.

Every time the sight of something new startled a gasp from her lips, regret rushed in. It felt like a betrayal, finding joy even in little things when Willow was in danger.

Luna's stomach broke the silence at last. Benny turned toward her and sat facing the stern while he handed her honey cakes one at a time. The smile on his face said, pure and simple, those honey cakes came with a price. And his price was answers.

"So you're going to find a doctor?"

Luna grimaced. "And how do you know that?"

"Not telling. I hitched a snare to your front door so I'd know when you left." Benny leaned back and flashed a self-satisfied smile. "Really, I should be the one mad at you for even thinking of going without me!"

Luna snorted. It *was* a supremely stupid thing she was doing. And if the brief history of her life was any indication, if she was set on doing a supremely stupid thing, it was best to have Benny along.

6

Perdita

The little family floated in a banana leaf boat they had made for the day. Perdy stood at the helm, grasping the stem in one hand and swatting droplets of water out of the air with the other. Gia lay on her back and stared at the clouds in the sky as they shifted and shaped into globs that almost looked like a bird's beak, or a blooming flower, or a skink sunning itself on a rock. Their mother lifted a hollow reed to her lips and blew, a stream of bubbles bursting below the surface and sending the leaf swaying across the water.

Gia giggled at the sound every time, and Perdy brightened every time Gia laughed.

"Why do we have to go?" Perdy asked her mother, abandoning her post at the bow of the boat to lay her head on the pillow of Gia's arm. "The humans leave us alone. The river is lovely. The fish and the birds and the bugs are as friendly as could be."

Mother clucked her tongue. "You know the answer to that, Perdita. Whether they will it or not, as the humans grow, we ebb. There was a time when we were friends with the humans, when we did not hide ourselves from them and we shared our magic with them. Before they dug down in the earth and brought the deepest, darkest metals out to taste the air, to poison everything they touched.

"Now this world cannot hold us both. If we wait too long, we may not have enough strength to make a door at all. We may not ever be able to leave. As it is, we can only make the one door, and hold the space between worlds open for a few minutes."

Perdy's lips pursed together. Gia took a knot of her hair, unwound it, and wound it back up with a sprig of flowering vine tucked between the plaits.

"You'll see," Mother assured her. "The fish will be just as friendly, and the waves just as fresh in the new world the door makers find for us."

"And we'll be together," Gia said. "That's all that

matters. When we get to this new place, I'll help you map our new stream. I'll go with you to learn the rhythm of the new rapids and the taste of the new lake. It will be an adventure—just what you love best. You'll see."

But still Perdy was uneasy. So she decided to craft a thing to take with them so they never really had to leave this place behind. One for her, and one for Gia.

Perdy wove a pair of coronets out of burnished fig roots. Into the wood she set crystals from the mountain streams, agates from the salty mudflats, and iridescent snail shells that glowed with the memory of the deepest depths of the lake. Every night, while they listened to the chanting of the door makers, Perdy wound a new treasure into the coronets. Every morning she emptied her pockets and set out again to search for that one last piece.

"Perdy, will you stop this wandering?" Gia pleaded. "You heard Mother. The door will open and *close* any day now. You have to be here when it does."

"I can skate all the way from the lake and back faster than you can blink. There's no way I'll miss it."

"Quit being so stubborn!"

"Quit being such a worrier!"

Gia stomped away. She didn't understand what it

was that called her sister away again and again, farther and farther from home. But there was no stopping Perdy, so Gia set out to find a way to bring her back again if she ever went too far.

She studied, and she listened, and she worked at the curious tangle of sprite magic. Gia watched the hands of the door makers and counted the phrases that passed through their lips as they fashioned the door in the air and probed the worlds beyond.

Perdy had no interest in such a still task; she had no discipline to work at a tangle that did not easily come loose in her fingers. But Gia was a patient soul. She wasn't looking for the same kind of magic the door makers worked. What she needed to know, what she wanted to master, was the coming home, the calling to the nest kind of magic.

The door makers were too busy at their task to teach what they knew—there would be time for that in the next world, they said. So Gia had to work it out on her own. First, she spelled a leaf so she could drop it anywhere in the stream and it would find its way back to the sandy spot where she waited. Next, she magicked a beetle to come whenever she called from wherever she called.

But it is one thing to cast one's will over a leaf or a bug; it is another to compel a creature with a mind of her own. What Gia needed was something even stronger, a magic powerful enough to carry her sister back to her. She cast around herself for the things of this world that she knew. She settled on the reeds that grew in the shallows of the river, that grew tall despite the freshwater crabs that tunneled between their roots and the fickle winds that flattened them at will. She stripped the reeds of their brittle husks and wove a belt to cinch around Perdy's waist, whispering her words of binding and holding and calling home as she worked.

"Do I have to wear this all day long?" Perdy complained when Gia knotted the belt. "The reeds prickle my skin. I'm going to get a rash, you know."

But wear it she did. And when that didn't work, she wore an eye mask made of spider silk. And when that didn't work, she wore anklets of braided leaf veins.

Gia's many tries and many failures sent her looking in places that would have alarmed the door makers and worried her mother. But her unusual methods produced unusual results. She discovered that not all of the humans' metal was a drain.

One kind, at least, fed her will.

Silver burned the tips of her fingers where she touched it, an icy burn that sent a chill rippling along her skin. Gold rattled the bones at the back of her neck like a teacup in a timid hand. Iron she couldn't even stand to be in the same room with. Not if she didn't want her head split apart with an ache that lasted three days, at least, and left her feeling drained as a tidal marsh emptied by the sea.

She felt like a thief, wandering unseen through the humans' huts and rifling through their things. But her need to find an answer was stronger than her remorse. As she scrambled to the porch of a hut planted squarely in the center of the meadow, she was nearly trampled when a young girl ran out the door. Gia pressed herself against the railing, shrinking out of the way and out of sight.

The girl spun in the meadow to face the hut again, hands on her hips. "Hurry *up*, Tin!" she shouted.

A boy with pudgy legs stumbled onto the porch. "Wait for me!" When the girl only turned away from him, running straight for the river, he called out again, wailing this time. "Tu, Mama said I get to come!"

Once the human children had gone, Gia stepped cautiously over the lintel, peering around the simple home in case anyone else came barreling through the door. Humans were so . . . big. And clumsy. And loud.

Gia moved around the hut, peering into baskets and digging through drawers. Finally, on a nightstand beside a lumpy mattress, her hands hovered over a pewter dish in the shape of a leaf, and they did not ache. She touched the metal with the tip of her finger and it did not burn. Gia emptied the dish of its trinkets and hefted it in both hands. A strange sort of power thrummed though her, and all at once she felt that creating this thing she had dreamed up, this thing she so wanted, wasn't impossible, after all.

Gia tiptoed as she carried the pewter dish away, for she was truly a thief now. Before long, her arms were sore from their heavy load. A dish small enough to hold human trinkets was a giant platter in Gia's hands.

She took it from the humans' village and down to the riverbank to a bare patch of dirt between the trees. Gia needed only a flake from its side, so she whispered words of breaking and drew her finger across the tip of the leaf, slicing it cleanly off. She laid the piece down in the hollow of a grinding rock and whispered words, not of breaking this time, but of fire and change. The pewter melted from a shard of metal into a small circle with a shallow dip at its center. Gia lifted the little disc out with a pair of tongs and lowered it into the river. A cloud of steam rose with an angry hiss. Three more metal flakes melted and were formed into three more discs. To each pair, she attached a hinge and a clasp.

The circles fit together, and they clicked as one half

met the other. A pair of lockets, but not with portraits inside or wisps of cherished hair; these, when opened, would be like doors of their own. Private doors through which to call a lost thing home.

And not exactly a lost thing, either.

The lockets, if the words Gia spoke over them worked as they should, would have the power to call Perdy back to her.

Perdy waited for her sister, the coronets tucked out of sight behind her back. Minnows swam in frenzied circles around her legs, flashing and scattering the light off their silvery backs. Gia waded out to meet her in the shallows. She too held a gift for her sister in her hand. She too wore a smile brimming with secrets.

Perdy couldn't wait. She pulled out one of the coronets and set it on Gia's head. The circlet was the rich brown of burnished wood, and it sparkled with the weight of hundreds of tiny treasures.

"There," Perdy said. "The best of every place I have ever been." She settled her own coronet on her brow. "Now we can go. Now we can step through the door to the next world without leaving this one behind."

Gia kissed her sister's cheek. "It's perfect, Perdy."

She fastened her own gift, a feather-light chain,

around Perdy's neck. At the end of the chain, a locket rested against Perdy's skin, as if it was always meant to be just there.

"Is this magicked too?" Perdy asked as she lifted the locket to study the markings etched into its surface. "Much better than that scratchy reed belt."

"Much better," Gia said as she fastened a matching locket around her own neck. "Open it."

Perdy clicked open the clasp and peered inside. Where dull metal should have been, her sister's face swam in a swirl of white clouds. Perdy looked up in wonder. Inside the locket, and there right in front of her, were mirrored images of the same rising eyebrows, the same upward curving grin, framed by a dense jungle backdrop.

"It's really you in there?"

"It's really me," Gia answered. "Wherever you are, no matter how far you wander, now I can always call you back to me."

"Gia," Perdy breathed. She closed the locket and cupped it between her hands. She darted forward and kissed her sister, once on each cheek.

"At full noon, when the sun is at its highest, open your locket. I'll open mine at the same time."

Perdy eyed her twin. "And just what is going to happen then?"

"You'll see," said Gia with a sparkle in her eye and a pinch more confidence than she actually felt.

So the sisters went their own ways, as they always did in the afternoons. Gia watched the door makers. The intensity of their search had picked up in the past few weeks—maybe at last they had found someplace to hold them all, a place that was still green and free and untainted.

Perdy wandered upriver this time. She'd heard whispers of a new spring—an undiscovered spring—in the jungle beyond the lake. She'd heard that the water bubbling out of that stream was pale as a newborn cloud and silky as duckling down. And she had a hunch that she knew just where this secret spring might be. So she skated up the river, around the crimped ribbon bends, and over the shimmering surface of Dindili Lake. She dodged the humans' floating city, the film that clung to the edges of their barges and weighed down their bristling lengths of rope with iridescent poison.

She followed the streams down to the rocky bottom of the lake where ice-cold water floated up to the surface. She followed them as they narrowed and crept uphill to the bubbling holes in the rock, where they squeezed through to kiss the air, to greet the bugs and the twigs and the dusting of seed pods they claimed as passengers.

Perdy touched her fingers to the locket that lay against her skin and tilted her head up. It would be an hour at least before the sun rose to the middle of the sky. She darted a look to the left, and to the right, and pulled herself, with prying arms, through the crevice in the rock.

The light winked out as she tunneled through the water, through the tight space the spring had carved into the stone, and down into the ground. She swam through the dark until a shiver shook through her, from the crown of her head to the tips of her toes.

All at once, the darkness didn't feel like an adventure. It seemed to press in on her from all sides, squeezing the breath from her chest. She laid a hand on her heart.

Thump thump.

(*Thump thump.*)

Thump thump.

(*Thump thump.*)

It was faint, but the sound of her sister's heartbeat, echoing from far, far up the stream, rippled through her. The feeling of dread, of darkness consuming her and never letting go, ebbed.

Perdy pushed forward. It was only around another few bends in the tunnel that a crack in the bedrock split the stream of water in two. The first channel dove down, where it fed, far below the ground, into the lake. Perdy veered upward, following the second channel toward a distant hint of light. She paddled and kicked, steadily rising until at last she broke through the water into the sunlight again.

She gulped the air and blinked, drinking in the daylight, reveling in the feeling of the air against her skin. The spring bubbled up, but only for a few feet before it sank below, then rose to the surface again a few feet farther down the slope, like a sea serpent's spine rising and disappearing again from view.

Perdy had found the secret spring—but her triumph was tainted by the taste lingering on her tongue of that close darkness swallowing her up. She didn't dive back down, didn't revel in her discovery. She cupped her hand, dipped it into the cool, clean water, and lifted it to her lips for a long drink.

Perdy turned her back on the spring and hopped down the serpentine stream back to the open lake, where the sun's brightness gilded everything in sight. She floated on top of the water, soaking in the not-a-cloud-in-the-sky warmth. She opened the locket and looked inside. Nothing. She checked the angle of the sun. It was almost full noon.

She didn't really believe this charm would work any

better than the anklet or the eye mask or the scratchy reed belt. But still, Perdy waited.

The ripples of lake water cradled and rocked her. Curious fish nibbled at her toes and leaped out of the water, arcing over her, one after another, until the last twinges of that cold, dark place drained out of her and she laughed outright, trailing her fingers along the smooth scales and gossamer fins of her friends.

A flash of white called her attention away and she lifted the locket up to her eyes. Wisps of clouds began to form inside, whirling and twisting within that small space. Gia's face appeared out of the mist. She smiled, and that same smile, in the space of a single breath, spread over Perdy's own lips.

Gia spoke a word Perdy did not recognize. Perdy listened, and with a *bang* she was pulled into the swirling clouds. The lake faded behind her and for a single, suffocating breath, she was enveloped in whiteness. Then with a second *bang* she was herself again, and staring into the swirling white clouds in her locket.

Only she wasn't on the lake anymore. She was standing on the rounded root of a seraya tree, shoulder to shoulder with her sister, who jumped up and down and crowed with glee.

"It worked! It worked!"

Perdy darted a look around her. There was the river, and the meadow dotted with the humans' huts. At the edge of the jungle, the door makers were bent over their work. Perdy closed her locket with a resonant *click*. "You called me here—with a single word—through this locket?"

Gia nodded, and her smile was brighter than any sunlight Perdy had ever seen. Gia gathered her sister's hands into her own. "Now you can never wander so far that I can't bring you back to me."

7

Luna

When the sun rose straight overhead, the river grew fat and lazy as a pig in a pen, and Luna slid her boat onto the wide waters of Dindili Lake.

All around the edges of the lake, traveling camps hugged the shoreline. Boats zigged and zagged out to the middle to the floating market where a dozen barges were lashed together, connected by bamboo walkways and patchwork docks. People who lived on the lake tied their boats to the sides of the barges like cattle birds hitching a ride through the marshland on a cow's flank.

"I've never seen so many people!" Benny cried.

"I've never seen so many boats!" As the bottom of

the lake sank out of reach beneath her, Luna gripped her pole and carefully stowed it between her feet.

"Your turn," she said, handing a paddle flat as a porpoise's tail to Benny and casting her eyes around the lake. There were flat-bottomed skiffs like hers, stubby punts dragging fishing nets, and ships built with steep keels, rigged with sails rising from the decks like fanned wings about to take flight.

Benny dipped the paddle in and out of the water, first on one side, then on the other. Clear, ice-cold lake water dripped onto his knees and ran down his shins, puddling around his feet. The farther he paddled from the shoreline, the bigger the swells of water grew. The wind picked up, and the waves crashed into one another, setting the little boat to rocking and pitching. Luna grabbed the other paddle and held it like a rudder, pushing against the water to keep the boat upright when it listed too far to one side.

When at last they reached the docks, Luna and Benny were both shivering and wide-eyed, goose bumps standing the hair straight up on their arms and legs. Benny jumped out first. He carried the bowline with him and knotted it tight to one of the cleats lining the dock. Then he knelt down, steadying the side while Luna handed their bundles up and hopped out after him.

They could have rushed off straight from the boat and into the milling crowd, but instead they sat for a while, letting the sun warm their skin and the gentle bumping of the dock against the barge against the next dock shake loose the last of their jitters. Benny opened his pockets, and they ate smoked fish and honey cakes and took turns dipping their fingers into a jar of coconut pudding and sucking the gooey sweetness off their fingers. Their toes dangled into the lake and they kicked up arcs of clean, cool water, the sunlight dancing around the edges of each drop.

"Luna, what if this doctor can't help Willow?"

"She has to," Luna said. "She just has to."

A quarter of an hour later, they shook the stiffness out of their legs and the crackles out of their ankles, and started down the walkway to the first of the massive barges. Luna clamped her fist around her jangle of coins as they wove through aisles lined with food carts and flower sellers, woodworkers' stalls and ironworkers' forges, past leering clockwork puppets and chickens clucking in their crates.

If she had come with Willow and Granny Tu, at any other time, for any other reason, she would have ducked into each stall and tasted the treats in every cart. Instead, she stopped only to ask directions, and to yank Benny away from the firecrackers cart and from a game of kick-the-can that had sprung up in a pair of abandoned stalls.

At the north end of the third barge, the heady smell of poultices and dried herbs led them to a hut with a swinging sign over the doorframe. It read:

DOCTOR AND MEDICINE MAKER:
PURVEYOR OF FIRST-RATE TONICS,
ELIXIRS, AND TINCTURES

The trip upriver had seemed to take forever, had frayed the worn edges of her patience, but now that she had finally arrived, Luna was afraid to go inside. She stopped abruptly, and Benny sidestepped to keep from running into her.

"Benny?"

"Yeah?"

"What if you're right? What if the doctor can't help Willow?"

Benny lifted the sack off Luna's shoulder. "Then you'll find another way. Go on," he said, sliding down onto the wind-washed planks beside the door, his mouth opening into a wide yawn and his eyelids already beginning to sag. "I'll wait right here for you."

Luna took a deep breath, and strode into the waiting room. Half a dozen people sat on cushions lining the walls, looking anywhere but into the faces of the other patients, as if even the knowledge of another's sickness was catching. The walls were covered with anatomical drawings. Luna flinched away from the sketches of skin peeled from muscles and tacked back from bones and blood vessels.

Luna sat in the corner on a mound of cushions where, through a curtain of strung shells and polished bone, she could see the doctor in the back room leaning across her desk and speaking intently. Luna's thoughts slid homeward. Was Willow awake and asking for her? Maybe she was feeling a little better. Did Mama guess by now where Luna had gone? Was she frantic? Was she furious?

The waiting room was warm and the incense strong; before long, Luna's head bobbed on her neck, her eyes drifting closed, and she slept. It was well into the afternoon when her turn came, and the doctor leaned over her, a chunky necklace dangling over Luna's nose as the old woman shook her awake. "Quick now, girl," the doctor said, and she brushed through the curtain. Luna followed, wiping the sleep out of her eyes and cringing away from the bone and shell curtain that swung in the doctor's wake, clattering and scolding.

The doctor settled herself behind a desk lined with jars and vials and a teeter-totter stack of musty books.

She steepled her fingers, resting her elbows on the pocked wood. "Well," she said, "how can I help you?"

Luna sat opposite the doctor on a padded stool, the fabric worn bare around the edges and the cushion lumpy beneath her. She pulled her fist out of her pocket and thrust it toward the doctor, the coins spilling onto the desk.

"Please," she said. "My sister is sick."

The woman held up a hand that was gnarled and knobby as the roots of a waterlogged tree. She leaned back in her chair and fixed Luna with an exasperated stare.

"Let me guess," she began. "You live on the swamp downriver."

Luna nodded, her brows furrowing together. People came to the floating market from all over—how did the doctor know Luna lived in the swamp? She rubbed a hand against her cheek. Maybe she had swiped some mud off her pole and onto her face that morning. It wouldn't be the first time.

"And let me guess," the doctor continued, "it's a wasting sickness, come on suddenly, lasting three weeks to the day. And none of the normal remedies will help?"

Luna nodded again, a wiggle of unease moving through her belly.

"Child," the woman said through a deep sigh, "do you really think you are the first soul to come to me to fix what clearly has not a thing to do with medicine?"

Luna swallowed. What was she saying? That she couldn't help? That Luna had come all this way for nothing? "But the sign in front of your door says 'first-rate.' It says 'medicine maker.' Make me a medicine!"

"Medicine is no good where magic has been worked."

"But I have money." Luna's voice climbed high as the cobwebs dangling from the rafters.

The doctor only shook her head.

"You're a liar, that's what you are!" Luna yelled, and her face flamed with heat. The ground seemed to sway and buckle beneath her feet, though she knew that so many barges lashed together were steady as a plot of land. "You're nothing but a liar!"

The doctor closed Luna's fingers over her coins and stood, waving the girl through the clattering curtain. "I can't help you or anyone else within reach of that cursed swamp. I am sorry, child. But that's that. You'd best get home and spend what time you have left with your sister."

The doctor backed her out of the shop, but Luna held the old woman's eyes until the weathered door closed in her face.

"I don't believe in curses."

8
Perdita

Perdy was high in the branches of an old seraya tree when the first of three tones sounded, low and resonant. It skimmed along the top of the water, through the clouds, and between mossy tree trunks. For a breath, nothing moved. And then suddenly the air was full. Sprites ducked under low-lying branches and dove out of passing clouds. They bobbed up to the surface of the river, water draining from their hair and limbs and staining their footprints. All the sprites converged on the door in the air that hung wide open, a gauzy whiteness filling the space between this world and the next.

Perdy was in a tree because she could no longer hold

back her curiosity about the wood sprites and their easy dance at the top of the canopy, skipping from treetop to treetop like stones across the surface of the water. What she had discovered, though, was that her legs, so well-suited to frog kicks through the water and to skating from wavelet to wavelet without breaking through the surface, didn't know the way a twig bends under pressure and snaps back once it has been released, the way some leaves hold a body up, while others drop out of the sky at the slightest touch. She could make her way up easily enough; like a squirrel, she had hugged the ridges of bark all the way to the top. But coming down was another thing altogether. She could only manage slowly, stepping timid as a kitten from one branch to the next beneath it.

The first bell tolled, and Perdy looked to where the door hung in the air. Gia would be there, right at the opening, clutching the locket and waiting for her to draw near so they could step through the door together.

Perdy eyed the cage of branches leading downward. Why had she climbed so high? Why hadn't she just stayed in the river, where she could sprint from one end to the other as fast as a wink? Maybe Gia would call her now. Maybe she knew Perdy would have gotten herself in some kind of trouble and she wouldn't bother to wait, she'd just call her back. Perdy opened the locket and peered inside, searching for her sister's face. Only white, swirling clouds swam within.

Snapping the locket shut, Perdy gritted her teeth and jumped, skidding downward from leaf to leaf, falling more than anything, skimming beside limbs strong enough to squash her like a flea if she put one foot out of place. Her arms pinwheeled to keep her balance and her legs skittered beneath her, fighting to keep her body upright.

The second bell tolled.

Faster—she had to go faster. Perdy leaped from the twig where she had landed, leaped to the trunk and slid straight down, her arms and legs splayed out, grasping for whatever grip they could get. She cried out as the bark burned against her skin and tore the soft flesh of her inner arms and thighs. When she was nearly through the tumble of branches, with a view of the ground and the sweet, sweet river below, the raised scar of a limb lost long ago knocked Perdy out of her downward slide and sent her spinning through the air. The sky and then the ground, and then the sky and then the ground flashed at her as she spun, out of control, away from the safety of the trunk.

With a terrible jerk, Perdy was yanked out of her fall, and she swung wildly from a jagged branch. She dangled in the air, held up only by the slender links of the necklace Gia had made for her. Perdy thrashed at the end of the chain. The locket dangled just above her chin—if she could only flick the clasp open, Gia could call her. Surely she would call her now that the third bell would toll at any moment.

Perdy reached, but just as her fingers were about to grasp the gleaming pewter surface, the chain snapped and she plummeted to the ground. She fell, and the locket fell too. They tumbled through the air, together for a quarter of a second, and then the distance between them opened wider and wider until Perdy could no longer see the sparkling chain. The locket, more precious than any unexplored cave or undiscovered treetop, tumbled out of view.

9

Luna

It was late afternoon before Luna and Benny climbed back into their little boat and left the floating city behind. This time Luna didn't need to fight against the wind-whipped ripples on the water. The lake itself seemed to feel her sorrow, seemed to want to lie flat and let her pass.

The lake spilled into the river, and the river wound through the jungle, turning in switchback curves into the heart of the wood. The river, too, seemed to know the sadness that had taken hold of her, and it carried them like babes in a basket all the way home.

Luna's arms were sore from pushing upriver all

morning, and more often than not, they hung limply at her sides on the way home, her pole trailing in the wake behind the boat. Every few minutes, she halfheartedly lowered it down to the riverbed and shoved.

She had been so sure the doctor would help—would do something for Willow. Maybe Mama was right. Maybe there really was nothing to be done.

Benny hadn't said a word since they'd untied from the docks and drifted out onto the lake. But his shoulders hung a little lower than usual, his breath rising and falling in heavy sighs.

"She didn't even try," Luna said, startling herself when the words broke into the muggy evening air.

Benny swiveled in his seat to look at her.

"She didn't even try," Luna repeated softly. "Said it wasn't a sickness medicine could do anything about. She called our swamp cursed."

"Of course it is," Benny said with a twitch of his eyebrow. "Poppa says so all the time."

"Well, I don't believe in curses."

Benny pushed a slow breath through his teeth. "Is it so terrible to believe in something?"

Luna shoved her pole against the riverbed. "Mama spends half of her day in that chapel when she could be with Willow. When she could be with me. Granny Tu is always checking her moon charts and going on about curses and sprites. And for what?"

Benny shrugged. "Maybe it makes them feel better to have something to blame, and somewhere to place their hope."

"Well, none of it does any good. It didn't do any good for Daddy, and it won't do any good for—" Luna bit down on her lip and raised her eyes to the sky, blinking rapidly. "Willow isn't just going to get better one day because we all wish she would. If we don't find a way to make her better, no one and nothing will."

Crickets chirped and marsh warblers trilled as the two children drifted homeward. The sun floated toward the ground, winking through the trees and slinking over the horizon as if even it couldn't wait to be done with the day. The sky turned to silver, and motes of dust caught and held the last bits of light, dancing on the air like tiny winged beings.

Benny shifted his weight, his knee bumping against a bundle that rustled and clanked.

"What's that?" Luna asked. "What do you have?"

"Spinners and fireballs and a whole packet of comets for the Perigee festival. I got them while you were snoring away in the waiting room."

"Was not!"

"Were too." A smile flashed across Benny's face and faded just as quickly. "Don't tell Poppa."

"How can you think about firecrackers at a time like this?"

Benny flinched. "Nobody loves watching the firecrackers more than Willow. I thought at least I could get something to make her smile." He worried the frayed edge of his shirt. "Maybe that's all anybody can do for her now."

Luna stuck her pole in the mud. She shoved harder than she needed to, and she flailed for a moment, swinging her arms wide to right herself again.

10

Perdita

We can't leave without her!" Gia cried. The door hung in the air, the white clouds swirling faster and faster within. Sprites stepped through in pairs, their forms dissolving like chalk in a rainstorm as they passed into the next world.

"Call her. Quickly," Mother urged. She gripped the handspun bag that held everything they would take with them. Her face was pale, drained of its color.

Gia slipped her coronet onto her head and opened the locket, where the same white clouds swirled.

"Perdy," she whispered.

"Perdita!" their mother cried.

Nothing happened. No contrite face swam to the surface of the clouds. If Perdy was stuck somewhere, if she was lost, she should know to open her locket. She should know Gia would be calling her.

"Perdy, answer me!" Gia said, louder this time.

Nothing, still.

"Pelagia, we can't wait any longer," Mother said, her eyes scanning the hardwood jungle as if she still believed, even as the words left her lips, that Perdy would prove her wrong, would come sprinting toward them at any moment.

"We have to go *now*. We can't hold the door open for her, and we can't wait. The door will close when the third bell tolls, and we won't be able to open it again." Mother pulled Gia into the stream of sprites that flowed into the open doorway. Swaths of white swirled in front of their eyes, over their skin as they stepped through, a veil of fog between them and the world they were leaving behind.

"If we don't go now, then all three of us will be left behind. Perdita wears your locket around her neck. You can call her from the other side."

"Perdy!" Gia shouted as the locket fell against her

chest, open and waiting. She allowed herself to be pulled through, but only barely, so she would be right there when Perdy tumbled, breathless, through the door at the last minute, as she always did.

Perdy, where are you?

11
Luna

When at last Luna and Benny floated across the swamp and the little boat bumped against the stilts below Luna's hut, the children swayed where they stood, tired from the long day and from the way sadness, like clouds dragged low by the weight of water, hung heavy over them. They climbed up the ladder on wobbling arms and legs.

Across the walkway, someone peered out of the shadowed doorway to Benny's hut. A shout rang out over the swamp and doors swung open, torches flaring into a web of small fires.

Luna winced. "So much for sliding home without anyone noticing."

Benny's poppa dashed across the walkway and lifted his son into his arms. "Don't you ever, ever, ever do that again!"

The news was carried from hut to hut until it reached the chapel at the highest point in the village. The door opened a crack and then was flung wide. The walkways tipped from side to side, trembling as Mama ran toward them. She slowed from a run to a panting, rail-gripping walk as she pushed through the crowd that hovered around the children.

"Where were you?" Mama whispered when she was close enough to see the purple shadows under her daughter's eyes. She gripped Luna by the shoulders, her whole body taut as a hooked line.

"I went to the floating city to get some medicine for Willow."

Mama stepped back, her hands falling away. "Well?" she said, thoughts rippling across her face like water in a slack tide, pulled in two directions at once. She extended a cupped hand. "Let's have it."

Luna dragged her lower lip through her teeth. "The doctor said she couldn't help us."

Mama's outstretched hand smacked against her thigh. "I *told* you it wouldn't do any good. Why can't you just listen?"

A hollow, hot feeling cracked open Luna's chest. "Because you just sit there in the chapel and Granny Tu just stares at her moon charts, and none of it does any good. We've got to *do* something, Mama!"

Benny wiggled out of his poppa's arms and slid his hand into Luna's.

"Luna." Mama sighed. "Don't you think I would help Willow if I could?"

She didn't wait for her daughter to answer. She walked into the hut, her movements stiff, her shoulders tight as if she felt the eyes of the village bearing down on her.

Luna slid her hand out of Benny's, and his poppa hefted him up again and held him tight.

"See you tomorrow, Benny," Luna said.

Inside the hut, Mama bent over Willow and pressed the back of her hand against her younger daughter's forehead and cheek. Luna followed, backing into the shadow cast by the wooden screen, her eyes trailing Mama as she left the bedroom again without a word. Left and sank to her knees beside her own bed, clicking her prayer beads around and around again.

With a puff of tired breath, Granny Tu rose out of her rocking chair. The joints groaned, the wood creaking against the floor that held the hut up above the swamp.

She draped an arm around Luna's slumped shoulders and led her over to the bed, lifting the blanket so Luna could climb in beside her sister. Her wrinkled hands tenderly smoothed wisps of hair back from Luna's forehead.

"I should've known better than to talk about the floating city with you in the room. Should've known what a brave girl like you would do with that kind of information," Granny Tu said, clucking her tongue against the roof of her mouth. "Promise me you won't go off again like that?"

Luna nodded.

"There's a good girl." Granny Tu's voice was low and rumbling. "Your mama is just frightened now, that's all. She doesn't mean the things she says."

Luna blinked back the hot tears that threatened to spill down her temples and sink in her hair.

"Truly, Luna, she doesn't."

But the words slid off Luna's skin. She managed a wobbly smile and rolled over, curling as close as she could to Willow's side.

Luna woke late that night to the sound of whispered voices coming from the main room. Harsh whispers. Outside, the moon was thin as a fallen eyelash, waiting for its wish. Luna crept out of bed, across the patch of light that lay like a rug over the floor and peered through a crack in the screen.

". . . too hard on her. This is not her fault, you know it's not." Granny Tu pointed straight at Mama, her hand shaking as she held it in the space between them.

"I just—I look at her, and I see her father. I see the day he—"

Was Mama crying?

"I look at her, and all I can think is that I'm being punished. I know I am. First their father, and now Willow—"

"Hush, now." The voices faded as Granny Tu ushered Mama up from the table and into their bedroom. Long after they were both asleep, Luna stood there, her fingers looped through the holes in the screen and her forehead pressed against the chiseled wood.

12

Perdita

Perdy landed on her back in a pillow of moss, trumpet blooms rising into the air above her. The breath had been thrust from her lungs so that she could not cry for help, could not cry out for her sister, who wouldn't be more than a hundred steps away from her. Still gasping for air, Perdy rolled onto her hands and knees, her fingers searching through the pillows of moss for a hint of gleaming pewter.

Panic bloomed in her mind as her throat closed again and again without drawing in any air. Finally, her lungs obeyed and pulled in a great gulp of air. Perdy's searching hands stilled. The locket was gone, but if she could breathe, she could run. If she could run, she might make it to the door in the air before it closed and sealed the way to the other world, before it shut her out for good.

Perdy leaped down from the bed of moss. Just as her feet touched the ground, the third bell tolled. She ran, pumping her arms and thumping her sore, scraped feet against the dirt. She could see the door now through the trees, wide open and only just beginning to close. Perdy thought she could see a figure in the mist, a figure whose form matched hers exactly, whose heart beat in echo of her own.

"Gia!" she cried.

But the figure did not respond. Instead her head dropped into her hands and her tiny shoulders shook.

"Gia!" Perdy sprinted toward her, but the door was closing fast.

She ran even as the door shut on the air, the edges burning as it sealed the space between. Then the door and everyone who had stepped through it were gone. Perdy crashed to the dirt where a faint line of ash marked the ground. Only a hazy wrinkle of air betrayed that any magic had been done in that place or that anyone had passed through at that spot, passed through from one world into another.

13
Luna

Luna leaned over the railing outside her hut, chin in hand. Every so often, a breeze kicked up, spinning pollen and leaf litter above the black water and banging Luna's boat mournfully against the stilts below. The boat spun in idle arcs and collected spiderwebs; one or two daring creatures stretched their silk all the way from the charm tacked at the bow to the wide stern.

Inside the hut, Granny Tu tipped the rungs of her rocking chair back and forth, back and forth in a slow rhythm that could put the fussiest babe to sleep. She stared into the empty corner of the room, her moon charts open on her lap, a date less than two weeks away circled carefully to mark the coming Perigee festival.

Luna sat beside Willow's bed, wishing her sister would wake, whole and healthy. But Willow's eyelids were still, and only the slight rising and falling of the bedsheet showed she breathed at all. Mama had left early that morning, taking her frightened fury up to the chapel where it wouldn't lash out like a bent branch and strike Luna's already bowed back.

Willow whimpered as she slept, as if the very weight of her skin against the mattress was too much to bear. The tiniest things bothered her now; she who had never been one for complaining before. If Luna lifted the curtain to let a little air into their bedroom, the breeze set Willow to shivering. If Luna was too excited or too loud, Willow's head would start pounding, the hurt pinching the skin around her eyes. And when they slept, Luna could never lie still enough so the mattress didn't tip and sway and wake her sister.

Shouts rang out from the swamp just below the window, and Willow's eyelids fluttered open. Her arms splayed, turned weakly up. She winced away from the light shining through the open window. Her lips relaxed into a tired smile when she saw Luna, who scooted closer to block the light from her sister's eyes.

"Where did you go yesterday?" Willow asked, her voice thick with sleep.

Luna lifted a cup of water to her sister's lips. "Benny and I went to the city on the lake."

"You did?" Willow winced as she swallowed, her eyebrows creeping together in a scowl. "Hey, Granny Tu was going to take us together. You weren't supposed to go without me."

"I know, I know. I'm sorry, Willow. I wouldn't have done it if you weren't sick. I went to try to help you."

"Mama was *mad*."

"Yeah. I know." Mama could go ahead and be mad. Luna would do it again. She would do something twice as risky if there was even a chance Willow would get better.

"Luna," Willow said, her eyes skittering away, "did you find anything—any medicine?"

A fly landed on the window and knocked itself against the shutters again and again, trying to find a way outside. Luna shook her head in tight jerks. "But I'm not done looking. I'm not giving up."

"I wish I could go outside with you." Willow let her eyes fall closed. "Tell me what you saw today, out there. Tell me everything."

"A big gust of wind sent a thousand seraya blooms

spinning out over the swamp. I watched a line of ants carry off a round of flatbread, one nibble at a time, while Benny's ma and auntie bickered over whose recipe for coconut pie should be used for Perigee." Luna laughed, for Willow's sake, though it didn't sound like a real thing, like a laugh that had any teeth to it.

"I saw a pair of squirrels in a standoff. They were staring each other down like a serious fight was brewing. Then one of them would jump up in the air and the other one would scamper off. Ten minutes later, they'd be back under the same tree and the whole thing would start all over again."

Willow laughed softly, her head lolling weakly against the pillow. Her cheeks began to sag, the sides of her mouth relaxing as her eyes closed. The sound of Willow's laughter soothed the raw edges of Luna's guilt, her sadness, but it opened up a fresh ache, knowing that sound would slip out on the air all too soon and never come back again.

Luna knew she should let Willow sleep, but she had so little time left with her. It wasn't enough. It would never be enough. Luna knew she should back away so she didn't bump or bother her sister. But instead she leaned forward. "Willow?"

"Hmm?"

"I didn't mean to dunk you under. I'm so, so"—her voice caught and she swallowed, blinking hard—"so sorry."

Willow forced her eyes back open. "It wasn't your fault, Luna. It wasn't."

The wind moaned through the trees outside the window.

"I promise I won't stop," Luna whispered. "I won't ever stop trying to find a way to make you better." She smoothed the blanket over Willow's shoulders.

Luna wasn't afraid of getting sick. She wasn't afraid of dumping her boat in the rapids up the river. But living without Willow—imagining a life where her sister didn't get better—that grabbed hold of Luna and tumbled her under like a water lizard wrestling its prey.

She stumbled outside, running, her steps skidding and sliding as the walkways tipped and rippled beneath her. She ran up the hill, veering into the jungle where the noise of insects chirruping and birds chattering took over. The canopy muted the sun and dripped dew onto her shoulders and hair and cheeks, dew that mingled with the tears sliding over her chin and soaking into the fabric of her shirt.

14
Luna

A week slid by, a week given to sadness and regret. Maybe because Mama couldn't face the guilt and grief brimming in Luna's eyes, or maybe because she couldn't find space around her own guilt and grief, she and Luna may as well have been strangers—not speaking, not even meeting each other's eyes.

Things had been different once. Granny Tu said so. Before Daddy died, Mama had been the first out on the water every day, quick to share a grin and a kiss, to snatch up one of her daughters and spin her around and around, high in the air, until the laughter of little girls pealed like bells across the swamp.

But sorrow can spread inside a person, blocking out any light that might find its way in to heal the hidden hurts. And so Mama went more and more often to the chapel at the end of the walkways, and spent more and more of her time at home wreathed in her pious quiet, in her grieving silence.

There were small things that could be done to make the sick person's time a little easier. So when Willow closed her eyes for her morning nap, Luna tiptoed outside. She passed Benny's hut and tramped along the walkways past the school, past the chapel where Mama had been since early that morning, and over the long bridge that led from the huts to the garden.

The trail zigzagged up the hill, and Luna put her hands out to either side to brush the tops of the ferns that lined the path and tickled her shins with every step. A solitary butterfly wafted out of the trees to settle on a cluster of orchids, while honeybees dipped in and out of the cascading blooms.

At the top of the hill, Luna opened the garden gate and fastened it behind her before stepping carefully between tidy rows of crops. Uncle Tin was in the far corner, kneeling beside a flowering cucumber plant and delicately nudging the spiraling tendrils onto the lattice behind it.

"Morning, Uncle Tin," Luna said, and she knelt down beside him, digging her fingers into the warm, dark soil.

"Well, good morning to you, Luna," Uncle Tin said in his leisurely way. "What'll it be today?"

"Willow's still sweating like she has a fever. She doesn't say it, but her eyes are all squinty, so I think her head hurts a lot."

Uncle Tin nodded as he listened, sifting through the soil with his weathered hands.

"And she still grimaces when she turns over, like it hurts to move at all."

"Mmm-hmm," Uncle Tin said. "Fever, headache, body aches. That sounds about right." He tilted his head to give Luna a sad smile.

Of course it sounded about right. Everybody, since the swamp first settled over the land, had shown the same symptoms. The same three weeks. The same helpless slow slide. Luna fixed her eyes on the ground in front of her, where a beetle struggled across the uneven soil. The dirt crumbled beneath him, and he fell onto his back, legs flailing as he struggled to right himself and turn his armored back once again to face the world.

"So, feverfew, right? For the fever? And basil for the body aches? And peppermint for the headaches?"

"My, but you're a quick learner." Uncle Tin dusted off

his hands and grasped the polished knot at the end of his walking cane. "Let's go look in the herbal to see if there's something I'm forgetting."

Luna helped her great-uncle lumber to his feet and walked with him to the garden shed where he kept his book of plants and herb lore. Inside, a small table was cluttered with jars of sprouting seeds and spools of twine. Spades and shovels were stacked in the corner, and rows of dusty shelves climbed to the ceiling.

Uncle Tin leafed delicately through the pages. "This book has been in our family for seven generations. It's got notes on tending the garden and taking care of the jungle. It's got warnings for how to keep from angering the sprites, from before they left, of course. There's even a little of the sprite's magic at the back," he added with a grin, "if you believe in that sort of thing."

"What do you mean, magic?"

"Oh, I wouldn't know. You'd have to see a sprite to ask it. And no one I know has ever seen so much as one's shadow."

"If you've never seen them, how did you know they were ever there at all?"

"You just knew. You got the feeling, sure as a body knows anything, that you were walking on land in their care. Anyway, the air is quieter now without the sound of their tiny feet rustling up the clouds. And sometimes I think the jungle itself is a little lonely.

"What do I know? I just tend to my garden. But some keepers of this book knew plenty about the sprites and their ways. Maybe if we had learned more about them, they wouldn't have left. Maybe, I don't know—"

"What is it, Uncle Tin?"

"Maybe they would have known how to help your sister."

Luna didn't want to say that he was talking pure nonsense. She didn't want to hurt his feelings. "We should have been the ones who left."

"Oh, a few families did when the sickness first came. But something went wrong every time, and they always came back."

Luna scuffed her foot against the dirt floor and kicked the legs of the worktable. A shower of dust settled over her hair and shoulders. She sneezed, and kicked the table once more for good measure. "Yeah, well, your stupid sprites can have their stupid swamp."

Uncle Tin chuckled, the sound rumbling low in his chest. "Everything is good for something, Luna. Even things that don't seem like it on the surface. Even the swamp that made your sister so sick.

"It's the silt from the swamp that makes our soil so

rich. It's the flowers that grow along the edges that keep the mouse deer and the honeybees close. I know it's hard now, but you'll see—no one thing in this world is pure evil or pure good."

The air in the shed seemed to whistle in Luna's ears, and a sweat broke out at her hairline. She collected the herbs and backed away. "Well, thanks, Uncle Tin."

Magic. Hmph.

Luna poured water over the herbs and set the whistling kettle aside. She cupped the mug between her palms and watched the herbs unfurl in a ponderous dance, the aroma of steeping mint rising with the steam to wash over her face.

Tap, tap, tap.

Benny peered in through the screen door, waving when Luna rose to meet him. "Hey!"

"*Shhhh.* You're going to wake them both." She jerked her head back toward the bed where Willow lay and the rocking chair where Granny Tu slept, her mouth open wide enough to catch a swarm of flies.

"It's time for you to bust out of here, Luna. Have you even seen the sun in a week?"

"I'm busy."

"Well, get unbusy."

"I can't go mucking around with you when Willow's not even strong enough to lift her baby finger." But Benny was right. Luna missed the feel of her push pole in her hands and the coarse belly of her boat under her bare feet. She missed laughing. She missed having something to laugh about.

"I'll tell you one thing: If Willow could string a scolding together, she'd tell you to get out of that sickroom and quit moping around."

Luna crossed her arms over her chest.

"Come on. You know she wouldn't want this."

Luna sighed. "All right." She slid past the screen door and stepped out onto the porch with Benny. "What is it?"

"The firecrackers for Willow, of course! Perigee is next week, and I want to set some off where she can see them from her window."

Luna rubbed her eyes. Perigee already? Willow's sickness would only last three weeks, and it had already been one—Luna ticked the days off on her fingers—one and a half. She swallowed past a hard lump in her throat. Her sister wouldn't live much past the festival.

"Okay. But I don't want to be gone too long. What do you need me for?"

"You take your boat out there in the middle of the swamp. I'll wait by Willow's window so I'll know what she can see and what she can't." Benny thrust a heavy sack with a rope and a float attached into Luna's hands. "When you get where I can see you, drop that in the swamp, so I'll know where to set off the firecrackers."

Benny went around the back of the hut while Luna climbed down the ladder and stepped into her boat, untying and shoving off in one fluid movement. It felt good to have her boat under her feet again, to feel the muscles of her legs flexing and straining to keep her balance. She thrust her pole into the mud and pushed out into the middle of the swamp.

When Luna was far enough away from the huts and the low-slung walkways, she turned in a slow circle and waved over her head to Benny. She lifted her pole into the air and Benny scrunched down until his eye line was level with the windowsill.

"Left, left," he mouthed, his arm jabbing in the air over his head. "No—too far—go back!" His arm jabbed in the other direction. "Right there—drop it!"

Luna dumped the sack full of rocks with its bobbing lead down into the water and counted the seconds until it hit and settled into the mud below. She tied the float taut so it couldn't drift.

Benny whooped, then clapped his hand over his mouth.

Luna rested her chin against the tip of her steering pole, looking out over the swamp at the clusters of swaying reeds at the edges and the trees half in and half out of the water. All that water had been part of the river at one time. Granny Tu said so. Maybe if it hadn't always been a swamp, it hadn't always been sick, either.

Luna took her time winding back through the trees and under the walkways, her thoughts unraveling like a ball of yarn, the fringes of an idea beginning to knit together.

"All set!" Benny whispered as her boat banged against the stilts.

"Yeah." Luna tied off and climbed back up to the porch. "Except I have to figure out how I'm supposed to keep the boat in that one spot and somehow dodge the firecrackers you light up at the other end."

Benny laughed, swatting away the idea like a gnat buzzing in front of his face. "Nonsense! It's going to be the best show of firecrackers you've ever seen!"

Luna grinned. Benny was right about one thing: Willow was going to love it.

"I've got to ask Granny Tu something. See you later?"

Benny nodded and backed away, down the walkway that led from her hut to his. "I'll be back tomorrow, and you're coming outside with me, even if I have to drag you."

"As if you could," Luna shot back over her shoulder.

But as she went inside, her heart felt lighter than it had all week, and the beginnings of a smile tugged at her mouth. She picked up the mug of steeped and cooled tea and set it beside the bed for Willow.

"Granny Tu?" she whispered as she tiptoed into the main room.

"Yes, love?"

"Do you remember the day the river changed its shape?"

"Of course I do." Granny Tu pulled a long breath through her lips, filling her lungs full enough to last the whole tale. Luna settled on the floor at her grandmother's feet.

"It was the best Perigee these woods have ever seen. Stacks of pies—banana crumble, sago swirl, coconut crunch—piled high as you can imagine. The day before, my mama set me to churning sweet cream so long that I thought my arms would fall clear off.

"The sky was bright, the leaves fairly dancing in the trees. And the moon, of course, was huge in the sky and white as freshly starched cotton. There was music and races and a thunderous firecracker show. Bright-red and golden-yellow waterfalls of light dropping out of the sky, their booms so loud it sounded like the very trees were falling down around us."

Granny Tu's eyes clouded over and she stumbled in the telling, as if her memory had wandered down a long-forgotten path.

"Then there came a sound like bells tolling through the trees. The ground shook beneath us, and what do you know—the trees *were* falling. We ran for the hilltop and watched from the garden as those big serayas crashed into our sweet, silky river." Granny Tu walked to the window, where she could look out at the swamp below.

"My mama said the ground just gave way. There never could be a better Perigee—even the dirt knew it!" The strong lines of her face fell. Her voice was softer and quavering when she continued. "Our river was so beautiful, sparkling and dancing through the meadow. You could kneel at the edge and see clear down to the stones lining the riverbed. You could dip your face in and drink, long and deep.

"But now"—Granny Tu shook her head—"it's all mud and sludge and bubbling muck." She turned away from the window, her eyes landing on Willow's pale, sweat-streaked brow. "No wonder it makes us sick."

15
Perdita

Perdy slumped between the trees where the door had been, where the air still thrummed with magic, where the last of the sprites had danced through to that other world.

Perdy picked herself up and stumbled back to the mound of moss where she had landed. She didn't know if the locket would work from so far away. She didn't know if Gia could call her from wherever they had gone. But she could hope. She had to hope.

On hands and knees she clawed through the moss, carefully this time, systematically through first one section, then another. When that didn't turn up even a glint of gleaming metal, she gulped down a panicked sob and fanned out wider. Maybe the broken chain had flung the locket farther than she'd thought.

Perdy dashed back and forth, searching, fear rising like bile inside her. Though her arms and legs were scraped raw, she climbed partway back up the trunk— maybe she could see something from higher up. Even in the full, near moon, the shadows grew, bleeding into one another. How had night fallen so fast?

Crickets chirruped mournfully as starbursts of flame leaped into the sky from the humans' celebration, lighting Perdy's path scarlet and golden. She stumbled to the edge of the water and let herself fall in, let herself be carried away in the winding currents, let the cool, clean water soothe her aching skin, her split-open heart.

Her mother was gone. Her uncles and aunts. Her grandparents. Her sister, in whom a twin heart always beat, echoing her own. Could Gia still feel it, so far away? Perdy lifted her hand to her chest and closed her eyes.

Thump thump.

Thump thump.

Silence.

Perdy's anguish rose from her throat like a wild thing.

Without knowing what she did, she called on the raw, unpracticed magic that every sprite holds within. It fed on her sorrow; it lashed out at anything in its reach. It felled the trees where they stood, and they crashed into the river, tumbling one on top of another, their leaves sticking like mortar into the spaces between the logs.

The river swelled and bulged over its banks, tickling landlocked tree roots and creeping to cover the mossy beds where wood sprites had danced just hours before. The river slowed until it no longer flowed at all, and the water swirled, furious and nervous, devouring the meadow.

Already, the felled trees were stemming the flow of water. Already, Perdy's treasured river was turning into something she didn't recognize.

She was alone.

She was lost.

And the locket—the one thing that could call her back to Gia's side—was gone.

16
Luna

Luna breathed deep the damp air that hung over the swamp and blew it back out of her lungs as hard as she could. Even the air seemed weighed down by sadness.

Her whole body itched to get out of the hut, to *do* something. But knowing the swamp was sick and knowing how to fix it were different things altogether. Luna quieted her breath and calmed her steps, slipping back to Willow's bedside. She set a checkerboard on the bed and lay down, chin in hand, where she could look up into her sister's face.

"I haven't seen Mama today," Willow said.

"She was here this morning. She kissed your forehead,

and made your soup. And you know she's been praying for you every second in the chapel."

"Is she still mad at you?"

"She thinks I'm reckless." Luna shrugged. "I guess she's right."

Luna clicked the wooden checkers stacked in her palm in a rhythm that kept time with her thoughts casting out and back, out and back. "I know she wishes it had been me that got sick instead of you."

It felt good to let those words out, to let the net slap against the water and sink slowly down. She shook her head when Willow tried to protest. "No, I wish it too. Every day I wish it had been my side of the boat that tipped into the water."

"I don't want that," Willow said, her voice trembling. "It shouldn't have to be either one of us." She gripped Luna's hand and squeezed hard until Luna raised her eyes. "Mama may not be seeing things right, through all that sadness, but she's going to need you when—"

"Don't say it," Luna said and she jumped off the bed. The checkerboard crashed to the floor. "Don't you dare say *that*. It's not going to happen. I am not going to *let* it happen!"

Luna threw her handful of checkers against the wall and ran out of the room, out of the hut. The walkway lurched beneath her. The sludge bubbled below and stars swam in her vision as she hung over the railing—the only thing keeping her from tumbling into the swamp. It dug into her ribs and cut her breath in half.

The stupid swamp that was taking Willow away. So what if it was sick—what could Luna do about it? How can you fight something so big, so sick you can't touch it without getting sick yourself?

"Benny!" Luna shouted. The door across the walkway swung open, and Benny stepped outside, his hair mussed like he had just climbed out of bed.

"Hi, Lu—hey, what are you doing? Quit hanging so far over the railing."

When she didn't move, Benny strode out onto his porch. "Luna, quit it. I mean it!"

She pushed herself upright, swaying. Their eyes met and held for a long moment. Benny didn't ask. Luna didn't have to say that it felt like the world was breaking apart under her feet.

"Mama made fried fish and rice balls, and tamarind cakes for dessert," Benny said tentatively. "Want some?"

Luna nodded, and he ducked back into the hut. A minute later, he stepped outside, a half-dozen tins balanced precariously in his arms. Luna and Benny sat on the walkway between his hut and hers. A breeze set the little bridge swaying, and they dangled their legs over the water.

They chewed in silence, watching the swamp swirl below. A water lizard slunk off a log until only his nostril slits and round, buggy eyes showed. Then with a flick of his tail, he dove below the surface, with no more than a ripple to show he had ever been there.

Benny shivered and pulled his legs back up onto the walkway. He turned out his pockets, dumping a pile of pebbles onto the decking.

"I've been thinking," Luna said. She stood and picked up a stick as long as her arm from the kindling pile. One by one, she tossed the pebbles into the air and, aiming for the gibbous moon already risen in the afternoon sky, swung her stick. With a satisfying *thwack*, she knocked the pebbles out over the swamp. "Do you remember what that doctor said—about the swamp being cursed?"

"Mmm-hmm," Benny answered, flicking the pebbles and watching them plop into the water, ripples spreading outward in quiet circles.

"Everybody always says the swamp is cursed, but Granny Tu said it differently today. She said the water is sick, just like Willow. I can't do anything about a curse. But what if I could do something about the swamp being sick?"

Benny bit the skin at the corner of his mouth. "When we were on the river, that water was moving all the time. It never stayed still long enough to help or hurt anybody."

"Exactly," Luna said. "If the dam wasn't here, if all the trapped water moved like it did when it was a river, the sick water would wash far away from here."

Luna tapped the stick against the side of her head.

"What?" Benny asked. "What is it?"

"Let's just get rid of it."

"What—the dam? How are we supposed to get rid of an old dam all by ourselves? And what about getting caught? Poppa's just barely beginning to let me out of the house again. Below the dam is one place I am definitely not allowed to go. And neither are you!"

"I'm thinking," Luna said. She turned in a slow, tight circle, tap, tap, tapping.

"I can see that."

Luna switched directions, circling the other way. "We'd have to dig the mud out from the underside of the dam somehow. If we dig deep enough, the water will slip through, a little bit at a time."

"Yeah, slip through right on top of us," Benny said with a snort, swatting at the stick. It spun out of her hands and landed on top of the water. "And then we're neck deep in muddy swamp water, and if we take even one sip, we'll get sick too. We can't help Willow if we're laid up in bed. And what if one of those trees came loose and smashed right down on top of us? No way. It's too dangerous."

Luna stopped her circles and hunched down beside him. "But what if when the sick water is gone, the sickness leaves Willow, too?"

Benny scrambled to his feet, the walkway tipping and swaying with his sudden movement. "Wait a minute. What if we weren't behind the dam when the mud broke apart? What if something else knocked it loose and we were far away, high up on the riverbank?"

"Something else?"

His eyebrows wiggled up and down. "A little explosion . . ."

"Right, because that wouldn't get us in trouble at all!"

"I'll just say I'm practicing for the festival. If we stick my comets into the mud and light them all at the same time, they'll blow little holes in the dam. And little holes, with the water pushing against them, might turn into a big hole."

"You're crazy," Luna said.

"Crazy brilliant, you mean!"

"Okay, but we have to light those fuses and get out of the way quick—far out of the way."

"We'll only get in trouble if it doesn't work," Benny said with a wicked grin. "If it does work, if we wash all that mucky swamp water downstream, we'll be heroes! And you're right—Willow just might get better."

"You really think a couple of comets will be enough to bust up the dam?"

"If it isn't, I'll still have the spinners and fireballs left over for the festival." Benny shrugged his shoulders. "And at least we'll have tried something, instead of just sitting around and watching Willow get sicker and sicker."

Luna nodded. "Tomorrow. Meet me under the dam at lunchtime. And bring your comets."

17

Perdita

At first Perdy was afraid to travel too far from where the door had been in case it reopened, pulling her through to join the rest.

But it never did.

She went back every day until the water covered everything, and the moss and whatever secrets it held were buried under layers of silt and mud. Perdy asked the fish and the frogs and the skinks to help her search for the thing she had lost, to search beneath the mud, to sift through the silt and comb through the fallen branches. But the locket was never found.

Eventually, Perdy began to lose hope. Sadness settled into the empty spaces inside her.

As the rising water loosed the dirt from around their roots, massive serayas with low-slung branches crashed, one by one, into the growing swamp. The dam thickened, week by week, month by month, as the trees lodged against the mud, mortaring themselves into a solid wall. High-kneed pulai trees sprouted in their place; somehow their seeds had smelled the swamp and had known which winds to follow to find the still water.

The humans could have left. They might have left their homes and walked up the hill or upriver to find new places to live and start new stories on higher, dryer ground. But most of them didn't. They stayed in the place where their grandparents had lived, in the homes where their great-great grandparents had first taken a felled tree and carved a boat to winnow through the streams.

Perdy went, sometimes, to watch the frantic scramble as the humans battled to keep their homes above the rising water, as they tried to pry the logs loose and cut out enough of the dam to make the river flow again. None of it worked, and after a time, they gave up trying. Perdy thought the presence of other creatures might comfort her, but it did not.

It only made her feel more alone.

If Gia were there, Perdy would have tromped through the thickening weeds and the water that spilled over meadows and swallowed logs. If Gia were there, Perdy would have greeted every new winged thing that buzzed over the waveless water. But Gia was not there.

The creatures tried to cheer her, tried to nudge her into their games as they had before. But after a time, they stopped trying. When the first snake slid into the swamp, Perdy hardly lifted an eye. When chains of moss grew together, she barely paused to run her fingers over the velvety links. She only dangled her feet in the water and sat, watching the space where the door had been. She sat still so long she might have grown a thatch of moss herself.

The wet months came and the swamp grew swollen, stretching wider and wider, until it didn't flow at all, until the riverbed grew thick with weeds reaching toward the sunlight and mud clogging every crevice. All around her, buds blossomed out of new green growth, gasping for first breath in the moist air of the trapped river. All around her, new life burst forth, and it only made the ache of all she had lost even worse.

The dry months swept in on hot winds, and still Perdy was alone. The heat drained the reeds and drove the fanged frogs down into their months of mud-burrowed slumber.

Each season that spiraled by pained Perdy.

A year passed, and sorrow drove her down to the water, where at least the coolness soothed her skin and she could see the jungle and the space where the door had been.

By the second year, the trees where the door had hung groaned and leaned, their roots failing to stick in the wallowing mud, and they toppled one after the other into the swamp.

Perdy sank just below the water where the sun still sparkled and warmed and winked, where she could slip into the shadows if she didn't want to be seen. Where she could float right below the surface, watching the clouds shuttle by, watching the world, altered and refracted through the ripples above her head.

Perdy stopped wandering upriver, stopped listening to the wavelets splashing against the rocks. She no longer raced the water skippers and danced the pondering underwater dance of swimming turtles and sprightly frogs.

Nothing sparkled; nothing shone.

Not without Gia.

18
Luna

It was the second of Mama's rules never to be broken: *Don't go below the dam.*

The rule wasn't there for nothing. Luna knew that. The layers of logs and muck that made up the dam were all haphazard, flung together and held there by a wall of water. If anything shifted, those logs could come tumbling over into the dry riverbed below and crush anyone foolish enough to be caught beneath them. And if someone was *trying* to shake things loose? Well.

Benny whistled as he wound through the reeds that rimmed the swamp. He wielded a stick in his hands like a sword, stabbing anthills and swatting at the tasseled tips of tall grasses.

"Hey, Benny."

"Hey, Luna. You ready?"

Luna swallowed. "Yep."

She kept watch to make sure they weren't spotted, while Benny hopped down into the dry riverbed, hands on hips, studying the dam that stretched high over his head. It was mostly mud, to look at it, with a few rocks and sticks poking out of the dirt.

"I think the mud's thicker at the sides, and at the bottom," Benny said, swinging his arm in a circle at the heart of the dam. "So we should stick the comets here, right in the middle."

"You're the firecrackers expert."

Benny dug divots into the mud with the end of his stick and wedged the firecrackers in until all that showed were twisted wicks hanging expectantly downward. All told there were five, arranged in a frown, right at the heart of the dam. When Benny was happy with the way he'd placed all the little bombs, Luna dropped over the lip of the old riverbank. Her legs slipped out from under her and she fell in a tumble of rocks and grit to the dry riverbed.

Benny dusted off his hands and helped her up. "You're worried. Don't be worried, Luna."

She shook her head; her lips pressed together in a thin, white line. "I'm not worried."

"Look, it'll be easy. You take these matches and light those two right there, closest to the riverbank. I'll light these three at the far end, and I'll be right behind you."

"Why do you get the risky part? It's my sister we're doing this for. It's my fault we're in this mess at all."

"Yeah? Well, they're my firecrackers. Besides, it's my turn to be the reckless one," Benny said with a wink.

Luna's hands shook, just a little, just enough that the pink tips of the matches wobbled in the air. She stood in front of her two wicks and waited for Benny. He arched an eyebrow and lifted his shoulders in a shrug.

"Ready or not," he said, and he struck his first match. It crackled to life, and Luna hurried to light hers. She cupped her hand around the wobbling flame and lifted it to the wick.

"Come on, come on, come on," she whispered. The flame danced around the wick, tickling all the edges before a thread of smoke rose into the air and the fibers whooshed into flame. The smell of singed peppers filled her nostrils as the match burned down, too close to Luna's fingers, and she hopped from foot to foot, shaking the match in the air and blowing it out.

The flame crackled as it ate up the wick, burning fast

toward the mud. Luna struck her second match and it popped into flame. Beside her, she could hear first one, then two of Benny's wicks begin sizzling toward their firecrackers.

"Come on, come on, come on," she whispered as she fumbled to light the second wick. It flared to life, and Luna darted a look at Benny. He flashed her a smile as he shook the flame out of his last match.

"Go!" he shouted as he dashed for the riverbank.

Luna turned and ran. She clambered up and sprinted toward the trees. She looked back over her shoulder once, just in time to see the wicks fizzling down to the very nubs and Benny's exhilarated face peeking up over the riverbank. Just in time to see him stumble over a loose rock, scrabble for a handhold, and fall back into the riverbed.

Luna skidded to a stop. "Benny!"

BAM! BAM BAM BOOOOM!

Luna covered her head with her arms as dirt and hunks of rock flew into the air. Mud thwacked against tree trunks and a rumbling thundered at the base of the dam, a rumbling like boulders clunking against one another.

And then it all stopped.

Luna raced back to the riverbank. She couldn't see

Benny anywhere. Everything was coated in a thick layer of mud. The dam held, even though five craters as big as crab pots pocked its surface. Luna dropped over the side.

Her head was ringing. Her arms were scratched and bleeding. She could hear shouts coming from out in the swamp, people running toward her, yelling at her to get away, get out of the riverbed.

Above her, the dam creaked, like it was trying to find a new balance, like the water was pushing hard as it could against the weak spots.

"Benny!" Luna thrust her arms into the mud and waded through the muck, grabbing at anything solid.

"Benny!" she screamed, though the sound that reached her was muffled, as if she had cotton balls stuck in her ears. Luna spread her arms wide as she fished through the sludge for a foot, a wrist—anything. She slipped and crashed to the ground, landing on something solid and wiggling.

"Benny!" she wailed, righting herself and grabbing at the wiggling thing beneath her. She pulled and a wrist appeared out of the muck, followed by an elbow and a shoulder and a sputtering, mud-smeared face. Luna pulled until Benny was sitting upright. She wiped the silt away from his nose and around his lips and hefted him up, pushed him up and over the riverbank, panting for breath as she climbed up after.

Benny crawled on his hands and knees, hacking and spitting, and Luna thought she had never heard a more beautiful sound. He coughed, and big brown splats of goo dotted the ground in front of him.

Benny sat back, leaning into Luna's side. He looked down at the dam below, still shifting, still grumbling, but still holding the swamp in place. He looked at Luna, and at the stream of people rushing along the edge of the swamp toward them.

"Now we're really gonna get it," he said.

Luna laughed and threw her arms around his mud-caked body. "And this time I'm pretty sure we deserve it."

Benny chuckled, but it turned into a hacking cough as he fought to clear his lungs again. Luna helped him to stand, and they turned together to face the crowd. "I'm sorry, Benny," Luna said. "We never should have tried something so dangerous. You could've—you almost—"

Benny cut her words off with a wave of his hand. "We're even," he said as he leaned into her. "I won't dream up any more stupid ideas if you won't. Deal?"

"Deal."

19
Perdita

Perdy returned every summer when the moon was at its nearest and pulled herself to the surface of the water where the door had been, hoping and wishing that somehow Gia had found a way back to her.

The years folded, one into another, and still she was alone.

Perdy's heart grew small, and sorrow hardened it into a lonely, ugly thing. The still water grew thick with weeds, and light filtered less and less into the depths. As the decades passed, Perdy sank into the muck until everything around her was as dark and silent as her broken, blackened heart.

After so many years of being alone, of missing her sister's hand in hers, her sister's smile, she came to hate the sound of laughter and any reminder of joy. A fish that frolicked a little too close or a tadpole just grown into his legs that kicked a little too sprightly would spur the anger inside her, and she would lash out like the forked tongue of a water snake to freeze that joy in its place, to stop it from disturbing her terrible quiet, from rustling up feelings that were too sharp to bear.

So it was that before a handful of decades slid by, Perdy was not a creature she herself would have recognized had she bothered to look in a calm, clear pool of water. She had changed so greatly that even had Gia been near, the sound of Perdy's shriveled, wicked heart beating would no longer echo her own.

20
Luna

Luna walked between the huts and knocked softly on Benny's door. He answered, a mug of tea in his hands and a thick scarf wrapped around his neck. Sweat dripped down his temples, and his face was flushed pink.

"You all right?"

"Yeah," Benny said, puffing out his chest only to double over in a coughing fit. "Well, almost, anyway."

"You're not sick, are you?"

"Nah," he whispered, rolling his eyes. "It just makes Poppa feel better to stuff me full of medicine and swaddle me like a baby even though it's hot as blazes in here. How's Willow?"

Luna shook her head. She swallowed, but she didn't have any answer for him. "Did your poppa take away the rest of your firecrackers?"

"Yeah. I guess I deserved it." Benny shrugged, tugging at the scarf around his neck. "But it should've worked. That dam was all set to collapse—I could hear those old logs groaning and the weight shifting. It should've busted clean through."

"Good thing it didn't, or else you would've been sunk under a ton of water. What—a half ton of mud wasn't enough for you?"

Benny chuckled. "Poppa says it was probably the creature under the slick that stopped the dam from caving in. He thinks if the swamp turned back into a river, it would wash that mean old thing away. No more swamp, no creature to cast a curse. No more sickness."

"No more sickness," Luna echoed.

Luna left Benny's and walked over to the railing in front of her own hut. She rested her chin on her hands and stared down at the water below and at her boat drifting in lonely circles. Footsteps shuffled across the wooden planks, and her grandmother's hands settled on the railing beside her own.

"I'm sorry I scared you, Granny Tu." It seemed like all Luna ever did anymore was apologize.

Luna

"Just because your sister is sick, that doesn't give you the right to risk your own life."

The breath left Luna's chest like the last hot winds of the dry season. "I only want Willow to get better."

"We all do, sweetling. But the damage inside her is done. There is nothing you or I or anyone else can do except be here with her now while she suffers."

Luna curled her toes against the decking. "I just can't believe that. I can't accept it."

Granny Tu sighed, peering over the edge to the swamp below. "Did I ever tell you why I tacked that charm to the bow of your boat?" she asked, memory thick as syrup in her mouth.

Luna turned her head to the side, resting her cheek on the backs of her hands. "No, you haven't."

"I wasn't so different from you when I was a girl. I, too, had a boat of my own, though back then, our swamp was a river, and our boats were much shorter, much easier to steer. We had paddles instead of poles, and it was my job to gather fish in the mornings for our family. My little brother—your great-uncle Tin—was always following me wherever I went, always tagging along after me. Often as I could, I'd leave him behind. I was the adventurer, you see. I didn't need a little boy slowing me down."

113

"But you love Uncle Tin!"

Granny Tu's eyebrows raised, joining the row of wrinkles that stretched across her forehead. "Do you want to hear this story or not?"

Luna nodded, biting her lips.

"It was Perigee, and Mama was busy, so I had to watch Tin all day. I was not happy about it. For a few hours I did as I was told. I let him tag along behind me while I played with my friends. At dusk, we decided to have a tree climbing contest—something Tin couldn't do. So I left him on the ground, and we climbed higher and higher. We wanted to see the firecrackers against the full moon, glowing against the clouds with no branches in the way. It sounded like a grand idea. But I looked down, just as the celebration was about to start, and he wasn't there.

"I could see a long ways from where I sat, but no matter which way I looked, I couldn't see Tin. I started to panic, not because I was worried about getting into trouble, but because, for the first time, I could see what life would be like without his tottering little legs and his cheerful, chubby face. I slid down that tree fast as I could and started running.

"I checked our hut, I checked the banquet tables, and I checked the firecrackers station, where they were just beginning to light the matches. But I couldn't find him anywhere.

"I could barely see where I was going—it was getting dark fast even though that Perigee moon was huge on the horizon. I ran down to the river. I swear I thought my heart was going to jump right out of my chest. When I got to the water, the firecrackers started, and they lit the ripples in the river orange and gold and red—it was beautiful."

Granny Tu hesitated, and she dragged a finger over her lips.

"You'll think I'm cracked when I say this, but truly, the air was thick all around me—it felt alive. I heard what sounded like bells chiming through the trees, and just then a flash of light caught my eye. I turned toward it, and there was Tin, curled up asleep beside my boat. He'd dragged it all the way down to the river by himself—only a pile of rocks had stopped him from reaching the water."

Granny Tu's lower lip began to tremble.

"All he wanted was to be like his big sister. All he wanted was to be included by me. Going out on the rough night water in a boat he was too little to steer for himself—he would have gone under for sure."

She took a ragged breath, and her eyes focused on Luna's face.

"What happened after that, Granny Tu?"

"Well, I was a blubbering mess, that's what. I picked up little Tin in my arms and held him tight as I could. Those bells went off again, and above us the firecrackers pounded away at the sky. I went back to where I'd seen the flash of light that had pointed me toward Tin and I found that charm.

"It was dangling from a chain slender as a thread of spider silk. I don't know why, but I plucked it out of the reeds. By morning, the river was creeping toward our doorsteps with nowhere else to go. The meadow was underwater, the land turning quickly into the swamp you see now. For a while the water was still clear and clean, with the brightest skim of green things growing on top, green things that never could have taken hold in the rush and flow of the river. Green things that hid the growing darkness beneath.

"As the years turned over, as the swamp grew, it darkened. We forgot how to swim. Nobody wanted a dunking in the swamp. The water had turned sour. Some families left, looking for a new place to begin again upriver, but they always returned. It was like something— someone has been holding us all here."

Granny Tu turned her back to the railing, looking through the window to where Willow lay. "Call it a sickness. Call it a curse. Say that a wicked spirit had taken over the water. Say what you will. Nothing was the same after that day."

She passed a weary hand over her eyes, letting them fall closed, letting her mind drift along memory's path.

"When every attempt to break through the dam failed, and we settled into life in stilted houses over still water, we learned to make flat boats fit for the swamp. I tacked that charm to the bow of my new boat to remind me every day how fragile life is, and how precious."

Luna squinted at the charm that had always been there, winking at her from the front of her boat.

"I know you only wanted to help your sister," Granny Tu said softly. "And that is a good thing, but I don't want you to ever think of doing something so dangerous again. Even if we can't save our Willow, life is too precious for you to be risking yours."

21
Perdita

Thump thump.

Thump thump.

Silence.
Sorrow.
Darkness.
Perdy slumped against an upended turtle shell, the waterworn membrane soft as a slug's belly against her skin. Her underwater cave was dark enough to shield her eyes from the sun and empty enough to hide her from the frolicking of playful water snakes and idle waterbirds.

Moisture dripped from the damp rock above to the damp rock below.

She was alone. She was painfully, terribly alone.

Thump thump.

Thump thump.

22

Luna

Luna stared, unblinking at the ceiling. Perigee, the nearest moon of the whole year, would fall on the following day. Two days before Willow's three weeks were gone. Two days before the sickness would pull her sister under. Luna's eyes were heavy from sleepless hours and her pulse seemed loud as drumbeats.

Call it a sickness. Call it a curse.

Maybe it was all the same thing, only different words used by different people struggling to understand the sort of thing no one can comprehend. To Granny Tu, with her sprite stories and moon charts, it was a curse. To Mama, with her prayers and penance, it was a punishment. To Uncle Tin?

No one thing in the world is pure evil or pure good.

He had been talking about the swamp, but maybe it was more than that. If the swamp had been green in the beginning and full of living things, then it hadn't always been a thing to be feared. What had changed? What had turned everything sour?

A reckless, risky thought shivered through her: Maybe the water only needed tending, like the garden. Uncle Tin said there was magic in the back of his herbal. What if it was a healing kind of magic?

Is it so terrible to believe in something?

Luna didn't care what word anyone used—she'd believe in anything by any name if it would make Willow better. She leaped out of bed and tiptoed out of the hut, closing the door gently behind her. Moving quiet as a whisper along the raised walkways, she crept up the hill to the garden. The night was alive, the jungle animals hooting and calling out from the treetops. The moon, a sliver shy of shining full and round, was just rising over the hill like it had been waiting for her, watching her every move.

Luna slid through the door of the garden shed. She

tripped on a shovel handle, and a row of spades and trowels clanged against one another, clattering to the floor. Luna stood still as a statue, listening for an alarm to be raised in the village and watching out the window for torches to flare to life.

But the only sound was that of the restless jungle beyond the garden, and the only light was the moon's. Luna picked up the herbal and leaned against the window, propping the heavy book at an angle to catch the moonlight. She flipped through sketches of trellised vines and instructions on seed starts and lists of herbs and their medicinal qualities. She went all the way to the back, where the writing was oldest and tilted in a looping scrawl.

Each page had a title, a sketch or two, a list of ingredients like a recipe, and a few words to speak while spreading the herbs or tonics or smoke. Luna squinted at the words on the first page.

*A tonic to sprinkle around the edges
of a tended garden plot to discourage
the virility of strangling vines
and seeding worts.*

No. The brittle paper crackled as she gently turned to the next page.

*An incantation with which to
strengthen the very roots, trunks,
and branches of an ailing tree.*

No.

*A dram of flower essences for use in
the purification of soured water.*

A ripple of goose bumps washed over Luna's skin.

She laid the herbal on Uncle Tin's worktable in a slant of moonlight beneath the window and ran her finger under the words. There was only one ingredient listed: juice from the crushed petals of a bat lily.

Luna stepped out of the shed before the clanging alarm bells in her mind could stop her. The only bat lilies she knew of were in the thick of the jungle, where she never went by herself. Where no one ever went at night.

Go back to bed. Look for the bat lily tomorrow, during the daytime.

No. If she was going to do this, she was going to do it now, before the sickness had one more day to try to take Willow away from her. She latched the garden gate behind her and took the fork in the path that led straight into the jungle. Five steps in, the canopy shuttered the moon.

The faint light that marked the path before her quivered as the trees swayed in the night wind. Luna crept through the jungle, her eyes spread wide as an owl's to catch the barest glimmers of light. Shadows that might have been tree creatures or might have been only knots in the bark loomed at her. A rustling sounded behind her that might have been a snake in the grass, or a fanged creature dropping down onto the path. Luna's heart slammed against her ribs, and she broke into a run.

Branches raked across her cheeks and thorned plants drew blood from her skin as she tore through the underbrush. Luna reached a clearing where the moon shone through a gap in the trees, and she skidded to a stop. Her hands shook and her teeth clattered together, though the night was wet with heat.

The bat lilies clustered around the edges of the clearing, their long whiskers dangling into the ferns below and glinting in the pale light. Luna made an apron of her thin cotton shirt and reached for the petals that lifted from their stems as if poised for flight. She tore them off one by one until all the stems were bare.

Luna clutched her pile of flowers to her belly and ran along the velvet path through the jungle. A woody vine seemed to reach out and smack against her shins, and she tripped, skinning her knees and elbows and bashing her chin against the dirt. The petals flew from her shirt and fluttered to earth like the wings they had always meant to be.

It may have been Luna's fear of fanged and sharp-clawed creatures, or it may have been her fear for Willow that ripped the sobs from her lungs and spilled salty tears onto the cluster of petals as she gathered each one and tucked it again into her shirt.

She walked the rest of the way, shoving her panic down deep where it could not tear at her and carefully stepping around roots and liane vines snaking down from the trees. The jungle seemed calmer in return, letting her pass while it watched with hungry eyes.

Back in the garden shed, Luna closed the door behind her and leaned into it for a long moment. She lifted a stoppered vial off the shelf and wiped the grime out of a small mortar and pestle. She ground the petals one by one and carefully strained the liquid into the vial until it held a few drops of the bat lilies' essence. She pressed the stopper onto the vial and ran her finger over the words in the herbal, whispered them under her breath until they took up a solid, ready space in her mind.

The moon laid a trail of light out of the garden, down the hill, and onto the bridge that led to the web of walkways over the swamp. Clutching the vial in her fist,

Luna went first to the chapel. She leaned over the railing, lifted the stopper free, and let fall a single drop onto the water below.

"Luminis salveo lucis," she whispered.

She didn't know if this was magic. It was pleading. It was hoping. It was speaking the deepest wish of her soul and asking the air to hear her. The recipe didn't call for grit from the jungle path to taint the juice. It didn't call for tears to turn the flower essences salty. Maybe those things would ruin whatever magic might have been possible.

But perhaps not. Perhaps a grieving sister's tears are just the stuff of magic.

Luna jogged to the schoolhouse and to Uncle Tin's, to Benny's, and finally to the front door of her own hut. She let fall a drop in front of each. She whispered the strange words as the droplets met the water, the hairs rising at the back of her neck and sending shivers down her spine.

Luna tiptoed inside, tipped the vial, and let the last drop fall onto Willow's brow and slide back into her hair.

"Luminis salveo lucis," she whispered.

23

Luna

Luna woke to the sound of shouting. The late night laced with panic had weighed her eyelids down and seemed to glue them together. If she didn't pry them apart, she wouldn't have to leave the space where magic felt like the stuff of moonlight wishes and desperate tears. She opened her eyes to let the morning in, and the night came flooding back to her—the herbal, the bat lilies, her scabbed and sore skin.

Luna began to tremble, her thoughts flitting like a pair of spiraling birds, rising into the sky. She turned slowly around.

Willow lay in a tangle of sheets, her forehead slick

with sweat and her cheeks sallow and pale. Her leg twitched, as if it wished to turn over onto her side but couldn't find the energy. Luna scooped her arms under her sister's bony shoulders and settled her onto her side as gently as she could.

"Willow," Luna whispered.

Willow's eyelids fluttered open.

Luna lifted a mug of cooled tea to her sister's lips, and Willow's watery eyes latched onto hers. She swallowed once and turned her head away.

"I need you to try." Luna's voice broke. "You have to try to get better. I've tried everything, and I can't help you. *You* have to try, Willow."

Willow's eyes slid shut again. The mug rattled against the table as Luna set it aside.

"Please," Luna whispered. She laid her hand on Willow's skin and felt for the faint heartbeat. Willow's breath scraped in and out, in and out. Luna stumbled to the window.

People were strung like beads on a necklace along the walkways, leaning out over the swamp, pointing and calling out in wonder.

The swamp was *green*.

Not black, not silty and dark, but covered with a carpet of green so bright it seemed to glow. Benny and his poppa poled through the water. In their wake, the bits of green, growing things swirled and separated. The water below was clear as a mountain stream, laying bare the creatures swimming and slithering beneath.

What good was any of it? What good was magic if it couldn't save Willow?

It should have been me.

The thought came in on every breath and banged against her insides until it echoed each beat of her aching heart.

It should have been me.

Luna's hands dragged as she passed Benny's and the school, where she could hear the excited chatter as garlands of orchids were strung and vats of roasting nuts crackled on the coals, preparing for the Perigee feast that night.

The planks rattled beneath her as she swayed over the bright swamp bursting with new life. The walkway tipped upward and she leaned into the slope, her hands gripping the rails and pulling her toward the chapel.

Set apart from the rest of the village and anchored in the branches of a pulai tree, the chapel was quiet, and more often than not, empty. The roof sloped like the ears of a scolded dog, and the door creaked as she pried it open.

Luna blinked, her eyes adjusting to the dim light inside. Sure enough, there was Mama, kneeling on the bare floorboards in front of the altar and worrying the prayer beads between her fingers.

"Mama?" Luna whispered.

Mama's shoulder twitched, but she did not turn around. She did not stop her murmured prayers. She did not answer.

"Mama, I'm sorry about the dam. I didn't mean to scare you." The beads clacked together as they moved through Mama's fingers.

"I know you didn't. I just can't—" Mama rubbed her forehead. She didn't look up. She didn't reach out to clasp her daughter's hand. "Go home, Luna."

Luna swallowed, and spoke even though she knew her voice would dip and flail. "Did you see the swamp, Mama? Did you see the water—clean and clear?"

Luna's mother made a noise that might almost have been a sob. "What does any of it matter? We're going to lose our Willow. And then what will we do?" The prayer beads clattered to the floor and Mama pressed her face against the wooden planks, a groan sliding past her lips.

Sometimes grief can make a person blind. Sometimes a person can't see through her own hurt to the hurt she deals out to others. Surely Mama did not know, could not know how her words sank like barbed hooks into her daughter's skin. How they snagged, catching on thoughts no child should think.

Luna sucked in a ragged breath and ran down the aisle, banging out the chapel doors. It would be better this way, she told herself, breaking into a run before she could change her mind. The family just didn't work without Willow.

Maybe she couldn't find a cure. Maybe she couldn't wash the curse downriver. Maybe she couldn't string up the creature and make it answer for all the hurt it had caused.

But just maybe, it would take her instead. Take her and let Willow go.

Luna scrambled down the ladder, knelt in the belly of her boat, and shoved away from the stilts, away from her home. She hefted her pole and stuck it into the shallow water, lowering hand over hand, then raising it up again, hefting it forward and pushing down into the mud.

Mama had three rules:

Don't go past the bend in the river.
Don't go below the dam.
Steer far away from the slick.

Luna gripped her pole in shaking hands and steered directly toward the slick. When she was close, when the bow of her boat was inches away, she dragged the pole, slowing her speed so that she crept, bit by bit onto the still water. The slick seemed to tug at the underside of her boat, seemed to want to draw it under. Luna anchored her pole in the mud and gathered into herself a deep, quavering breath.

It was quiet, the kind of quiet that has ears to listen.

"Take me," Luna whispered into the quiet. "Let my sister go and take me instead."

The words fell on the water, licked the ripples that fanned out from the sides of her boat, and sank down in the watery way that sound travels in the beneath. Sank into a cave where a bubble of air was trapped against musty rock—a dark cave where a creature waited, so miserable she couldn't bear the sunlight, couldn't bear the sound of laughter or trilling birds or the hum of dragonfly wings.

The creature cocked her tiny head and listened. Even that little movement made her ache. But the sound of the words that floated down through the swamp pushed at her, nudged at her. So she rose to the surface, though every movement was a pain in her chest. She clawed her way slowly up to the source of the sound.

⊸∅⊶

Luna waited in her little boat so long that her whole body sagged, drained of all that had kept her fighting for those fleeting few weeks. She rested her forehead against her hands that gripped the top of her steering pole, the ends of her hair dangling lifelessly at the edge of her vision.

She had asked, and nothing had happened.

She had offered, and hadn't been taken.

She had believed.

She had done everything she could to make Willow better, and none of it had worked. Maybe there was no such thing as the creature after all. Maybe there was no reason for her sister's illness. Maybe it was just one of those things where no one and nothing is to blame, it just is, and all that can be done is to try to live through it.

Luna lifted her pole free of the muck. If she hurried home, she could slip back inside before anyone noticed she had been gone. She could wiggle under the covers beside Willow and hug her sister tight. They would have one last Perigee together.

Just as she began to push her pole down into the mud to steer her boat back home, a tiny hand reached up out of the swamp, grabbed hold of the bow of her boat, and pulled. Luna gasped as the water foamed up, spilling over the edges, over the charm that glinted for the last time in the light of the sun.

Luna squirmed back until she was pressed against the bony stern; she gripped the sides as the bow sank beneath the water. It covered her ankles, then her knees, her hips, then her ribs, her shoulders—she took a last, long breath of air and the swamp closed over her head.

24
Perdita

Perdy pulled and pulled, down through the swamp water, down through the tangle of slimy weeds. She pulled the boat, though it was twenty times her size, pulled the human with it into her lair. She dragged the boat up into the bubble of trapped air and onto the rocky beach.

The human was coughing, sputtering as she clung to the sides of her boat, sludge sliding off her hair and splattering at her feet.

Perdy sank into the pile of upturned turtle shells that propped her up like a queen in her underwater court and righted the coronet on her brow.

Perdy was tired. So tired. Pain shook through her tiny body and clattered her very bones. Something about this human rattled her insides, rattled loose the oldest, sharpest hurt inside her.

"Why have you called me?" she asked, the words scraping like stones sliding past one another. "Why couldn't you just leave me alone?"

The human licked her lips and spat out the grit she found there. "It's my sister," she croaked. "She's sick. Your curse has made her sick. Please take it away—please!" The human began to shake, skinny elbows bumping against pumping ribs.

"You can keep me." The girl looked around her at the wet darkness. "You can keep me here forever, if you just make Willow better."

"What would I want with a giant human stomping around the place and sucking up all the air? My curse," Perdy muttered. *"Pffft."*

The human's chin began to wobble and water leaked out of her eyes, rolling down her cheeks and splashing against the rocks. Perdy raised a weary hand to her brow. It was all too much. "Just go," she said. "Go and take your tears with you. Go and leave me to my misery."

The human was blubbering now, sunk to her knees on the sharp rocks that dug into her flesh and scraped the skin raw. Even on her knees, she towered over the little sprite. "Please," she begged. "Please take your curse away."

"My curse," Perdy echoed, swatting at the air as if she could squash the idea as easily as a bug. She slid off her falling-down throne and approached the human. "A curse needs passion to feed on—love or hate, either will do. What do I have inside me? Nothing. I have nothing, no one left."

The human eyed the water lapping at the edge of the rocky beach and the crabs skittering into the shadows. She looked at the dripping ceiling of the cave above her and at the miserable creature before her. She stood and walked to her boat half in, half out of the black swamp water. But instead of shoving off, instead of drawing a deep breath to carry her all the way to the surface, the human spoke again.

"What do I have to offer, if you won't take me?" Her voice trembled with the weariness of spent tears. "You want our hut? Take it. You want our garden? You can have it. Here, take my boat. Take it. Take whatever you want, just give me my sister back!"

Perdy stomped across the rocky beach and kicked the wooden hull. "Why would I want your stu—" The boat rocked the tiniest bit, not enough to send it back into the water, but just enough so the charm tacked to the bow gleamed for a second as it caught the dim light bouncing off the cave ceiling.

Perdy's eyes grew wide and she crawled up the side and into the boat, scrambling over the slippery wood to the narrow bow. She reached out. Her hand trembled as she pried the charm away from the wood. Her fingers skittered over the gleaming pewter as if they knew the shape of the thing they touched. Her mouth fell open and a sigh, full of the bleak, lonely decades, left her lungs.

Perdy's eyes narrowed even as her insides wrenched with unfamiliar hope. She whipped around to face the human. "H-How did you . . . ?" she stammered. "Where did you find this?"

"It's just a good luck charm. My grandmother found it when she was a girl. That's what you want? Take it. Please." The human crouched beside the boat and raised her clasped hands to Perdy, begging. "Please, just let my sister go."

With each breath, Perdy felt her limbs lightening, sloughing off the terrible weight that had held her down for so very long. She looked up. The human's eyes blinked wide; a question perched on her lips.

Perdy flicked the locket open. Her eyes spilled over with black tears that ran like tar down her face, black as a lonely, shriveled heart, black as agony, black as a curse. They ran until the black faded to gray and then to clear, salty tears. She looked with eyes bright as the day they were born into the locket, where a gauzy, white space shimmered like a trapped cloud.

Perdy spoke, her voice thin and breaking on the single word. "Gia?"

A face appeared in the clouds, and the white space reached out, wrapped around Perdy, and pulled her into itself. She looked back once to where the human crouched, staring at the locket, her eyes shiny with some great thing that Perdy suddenly felt too, a thing that she had not felt in such a very long time.

The cave echoed with the sound of two hearts beating rapidly together.

Thump thump.
  (Thump thump.)
Thump thump.
  (Thump thump.)

25
Luna

With a bang that rattled every bone in Luna's body, the creature was sucked into the locket. The bang blew Luna backward, out of the cave and into the water. It was loud enough to rumble the bed of the swamp and strong enough to rattle the logs that held the water captive.

Luna clawed through slime and sludge and the film of bright green growth at the top of the water. She gasped a great lungful of air as she broke the surface, sputtering and choking. A current whipped up and dragged at her legs, trying to pull her toward the groaning, bending dam. Sticks and logs and entire trees rushed past as, with a final, earth-shuddering crash, the dam burst loose.

Luna paddled and pulled, reaching for anything solid she could hang on to. But the water was too strong. With the pent-up fury of decades, it swept away everything it touched. In a last, desperate lunge, Luna stretched toward the leggy roots of a pulai tree. She kicked and she grabbed and her fingers closed around the sturdy wood. Her legs trailed in the water behind her, trying to drag her with it. But she fought back, not for Willow this time, or for Mama, not for Granny Tu or Benny or for anyone else. She fought for herself.

She had broken every one of Mama's rules. Even if it hadn't been enough to save Willow, she had done everything, tried everything she could. She still had Granny Tu, who loved her no matter what. She had Benny, the best friend anybody could ask for. Mama would come out of her grief someday. And they would figure out how to be a family again.

I did everything I could.

The thought gave her strength. She gripped the roots, wrapping her legs and arms around the tree, hugging tight as the water streamed past her, taking with it the last of her regret, the last of her guilt.

Inch by inch the water fell, inch by inch it pulled back from the flats, laying bare land where wildflowers had once grown, where mud now gurgled and spat, tasting the air for the first time in a very long time. The village trembled on its stilts, and the people clung to the railings as they watched the water roar past. It shook itself from its swampy, gritty dregs and drained into the dry river-bed, the water, at last, set free.

26
Luna

Luna clung to the pulai until the river settled on a channel between trees and stayed put. She shivered, as much from the chill of drenched clothes against her skin as from all that had happened. The creature was gone. The swamp was gone. Was it too much to hope that maybe even the sickness was gone?

In the time that it took for the sun to climb to the highest point in the sky, the river had rid itself of the silt and the muck, and ran clean and clear as the headwaters that gave it life. Luna's boat was lost. Maybe Granny Tu would show her how to make a new one, skinny with high sides instead of shallow and wide, and with paddles instead of a steering pole.

Luna looked around the bubbling mud that stretched as far as she could see. She slid down and touched her foot to the surface, pushed against it, trying to stand. With a *slurp* and a *pop*, her foot was sucked down into the muck. She yanked it back out again, and shimmied higher up the trunk.

She was stuck.

Out in the river a fish as long as her arm leaped from the water, snatching a mayfly out of the air and splashing gleefully back down. The huge Perigee moon had already risen a quarter of the way up, a pool of milk against a pale blue afternoon sky.

"Luna?"

The voice sounded far away and too high, too frantically high.

"Benny!" she shouted. "Benny, over here!"

Benny wove slowly between the pulai trees, his limbs splayed wide like a water skipper, shifting first an arm, then a leg, then another arm, and the other leg. His feet were strapped to a web of sticks that spread his weight out over the mud so they hardly sank in at all. He held two sticks like poles in his hands, with little webs at the end of those, too. Each time he moved, the web lifted out of the mud with a sound like a crab plopping into the water.

"Benny!" Luna cried. "I've never in my whole life been so happy to see you."

Benny slurped closer. "What'd I tell you? Perigee hero. It was meant to be!"

Luna laughed and edged toward the mud as Benny sidled alongside her tree.

"You sure those things can hold us both? I don't want to sink you."

"What, you think you're my first rescue of the day? Hop on."

Luna lowered herself onto Benny's back, and sure enough, the webs sank a little farther into the muck, but not too far. With a grunt and a few carefully placed steps, Benny turned around and slurped back toward the village.

"Benny, have you seen Willow? Is she any better?"

"I don't know. I haven't been to your hut yet, there were so many people stranded." He shook his head gently, so even that small movement wouldn't throw them both off balance. "Some Perigee this turned out to be, eh?"

She patted his shoulder. "I'm sure they'll still make time for the firecrackers tonight, don't you worry."

"Luna," Benny said in a voice that was pitched just a little too carefully. "What were you doing out there?"

Luna sighed. She didn't know if what had happened was a thing she could find words for. All her life she'd heard stories of the terrible creature below, but now she found herself wishing she could hold on to that look on its face just before it disappeared, that look of hope and love and promise.

"I met the creature, only it's not—she's not what you'd think. I watched the sickness—the curse—whatever you want to call it, I watched it roll in black tears out of her. She was . . . I don't know. It's a long story, Benny. A long, long story."

"You know you're going to tell me everything."

"Yeah, Benny. I know."

Luna laid her chin on Benny's shoulder and held on tight as he brought them steadily closer to the village. The huts seemed out of place, like too-tall waterbirds airing their bare ankles. Everything looked different. The place she had spent her whole life was a place she was going to have to get to know all over again.

"Benny, you little water skipper, you!" Granny Tu called, waving an arm over her head. "You bring that girl up here where I can give her a proper hug."

Luna laughed, but the noise caught in her throat. Mama ran out of the house and gripped the railing as she watched her daughter draw near.

Granny Tu nudged Mama with her elbow.

"You did this?" Mama asked, her eyes full of something buoyant and bright. "You drained the swamp and got rid of the creature?"

"Something like that," Luna said, her wince softening into a grin. "I did it for Willow. Was it—Is she—"

Mama got down on her knees and reached for Luna. The rushing water had left even the ladder high and dry, and Luna had to stand on Benny's shoulders to reach the bottom rung and climb. Mama pulled her up the last bit, and held her close for several heartbeats. Granny Tu wrapped her arms around the both of them. Luna couldn't see their faces, but she could feel the ragged pull of their breath, the heavy sighs that set their worry free.

After a time, Mama backed away and placed her hands on either side of her daughter's face. "Luna," she said, "I can't believe how brave you were. I can't believe I let myself get so wrapped up in sadness that I couldn't see it—I couldn't see *you*."

A pair of pelicans leaped from their perches and flapped, ungainly, steadily rising along the path of the newborn river.

With a gentle push between Luna's shoulder blades, Mama said, "Go on inside."

Luna walked into the hut and around the paneled

screen at the back, her heart swelling until there wasn't room for anything else, not breath, not speech, not fear or worry. Willow sat up in bed, her arms outstretched, starbursts of pink on her cheeks and a wide smile breaking on her lips. The sheets all around her were speckled with black sludge where the curse had finally sweated out of her.

Like the river that had been hemmed and penned in and suddenly set free, Luna ran to throw her arms around her sister.

"Happy Perigee, Luna!" Willow beamed. "Isn't this just the best day ever?"

Epilogue

The river flows.

It begins as a trickle deep in the heart of the jungle, in the thick, secret heart of the jungle. It surges and swirls, gorging on the breath of a thousand streams.

The river, it bells, and it swells, and it flows, and a reed-thin girl in a skinny boat spins in slow circles. Her sister perches at the bow, calling directions and captaining the little craft. The pair of them hold paddles flat as porpoise tails, and the boat skims along an eddy where a swamp once covered everything in sight. The sound of their laughter winds like chimes through tree roots reacquainting themselves with the air. It bounces off dirt drying in the midday sun and skips over the cool, clear ripples of water rushing past.

In another world separated from this one by a veil of whirling clouds, a second pair of sisters ride the currents of a different river just as silken, just as sweet. Arms outstretched, their fingers interlace, as if they cannot bear to be separated even for a breath. They are rocked in the wavelets while the fish below buoy them up on a pillow of bubbles. A thousand droplets leap away from the steady flow to kiss their tiny brows.

Mornings are born, evenings fade, and still the river slides by.

Acknowledgments

I am so grateful for my editor, Reka Simonsen, who is loyal and kind and so very wise! Many thanks to the wonderful team at Atheneum Books for Young Readers for welcoming me, and for turning this story into such a lovely book: Justin Chanda, Emma Ledbetter, Sonia Chaghatzbanian, Jeannie Ng, and Chava Wolin.

To my brilliant agent, writing partners, and early readers, thank you for your encouragement and faithful critique: Ammi-Joan Paquette, Meg Wiviott, Anna Jordan, Kristin Derwich, and Tiffany Crowder.

Finally, to my friends and family, thank you for understanding and embracing my near-constant state of daydreaming and plotting, and for making life in this real world so fantastic! I love you all.

TURN THE PAGE
FOR A SNEAK PEEK AT

THREE Pennies

In the musty attic of an old Victorian home, a slight girl knelt beside a leaded glass window. Light leaked up through the floorboards from the parlor below, and the trusses creaked as the house groaned, its weight shifting on the unsteady ground.

Summer in San Francisco is a foggy business, so while kids in other towns ran through sprinklers and flung themselves off rope swings into cool green lakes, on this twenty-third day of July, Marin stayed indoors.

She wore a striped cardigan over her bony shoulders, and thick cotton socks up to her knees. A single crease between the girl's eyebrows betrayed the serious nature of her business that afternoon.

Marin asked a question aloud, her thin voice barely disrupting the air in the narrow attic. She tossed three pennies onto the floor and peered into the small book that lay open in her lap, the spine so thoroughly creased at that particular spot that the pages lay open without complaint. She scratched a mark on a scrap of paper and collected the pennies again.

Six times she threw the coins. Six times she made a mark.

The fog rolled in and hung about the scrollwork eaves of the house, pressing against the attic window, as if it wished to see the *I Ching*'s answer for itself.

Owls are supposed to sleep during the day. Everybody says so. But an owl who lives in a big city sometimes gets confused about which light is the daytime kind of light and which is the night kind. And so it was that an owl who lived in the bend of a stovepipe between two high-rise buildings was awoken by blaring car horns and flashing headlights that marked the end of the workday. He blinked at the traffic shuttling below. Owl watched as people scurried up and down the sidewalks, and in and out of taxis, headed home for the evening.

OOOOoooo. He'd had a home once, too.

Owl remembered when he was just an owlet and the old man had found him at the base of the towering redwood tree out of which he had tumbled. His feathers twitched as he remembered the splint on his wing and the woven bamboo cage that held him until the wing was strong enough to test. Most of all, he remembered their daily study, and the pellets of wisdom the old man had shared with his little winged student.

Now that his teacher had gone, Owl wondered if he should leave the city for the quiet forests to the north. His wings wished to go, but his heart would not yet let him.

OOOOoooo, Owl thought. *OOOOoooo. The bird that chases two rabbits catches neither.*

Across town, in a beige cubicle within a large beige office building, Gilda Blackbourne stared at the stack of files on her faux wood desk. Her stockinged feet rested on the stained beige carpet between the tennis shoes she had worn when she'd walked to work that morning and the discount heels she wedged her feet into whenever she left her desk.

Gilda curled her toes, stacked her feet, one on top of the other, and sighed.

It wasn't her fault that Sheila had a nervous breakdown last Thursday and showered the contents of her desk drawer out the window and onto the sidewalk below. Or that Frederick had run off last autumn with the paper clip heiress he met on an Internet dating website. But though it never was Gilda's fault when her coworkers left their posts, invariably, their abandoned caseloads were added to hers. Believe me, there were many times when

Gilda contemplated feeding her discount heels to the shredder and ditching the position herself.

Gilda did not like shifting children from foster home to foster home like chess pieces on a game board. She did not relish protracted legal disputes and endless court hearings. And she most decidedly did not enjoy being called to remove children from the scene of a domestic dispute. But there was one aspect of her chosen occupation that suited Gilda exceedingly well.

The arm of the government that oversees the welfare of children who are disconnected from their parents operates on a system of strictly enforced rules. And Gilda Blackbourne was a rule follower in the extreme.

Far below the city, below the dirt and the concrete and the cars, below the buried skeletons of burned-out row homes and carriage houses and trolleys, below even the bedrock itself, two massive shelves of rock slid past each other.

The sliding was slow, not the slipping past of cars on a freeway, or ships through a drawbridge. It was the groaning, grinding sort of passing of two things that aren't meant to occupy the same space. Every so often, the sliding would jolt and scrape, and the city above would tremble and crash in response. The crashing was a release of sorts, a welcome release after all that time pressing and grinding together.

But it wasn't time for that release, not yet. Almost. Soon.

In the city above, a woman stood before a tall window, wishing.

Her work was good, important work. Her home was full of friends and laughter whenever she wanted it so. Her heart was warm, her life was rich, and yet . . . Lucy wished for one thing more.

She cradled her mug of tea in both hands and blew across the amber water. The steam spread out across the windowpane, clouding the rows of old Victorians and high-rise apartments dotted with yellow-lit windows and filled with busy families talking around dinner tables and bickering over things like television remotes or grocery lists or what board game to play that night.

Lucy didn't look over her shoulder and down the hallway to the closed door with the cut crystal handle. Instead, she watched as the steam on the windowpane slowly receded around the edges and the city flared into focus.

She watched, and she wished.

O ver the years, Marin had discovered several rules for survival in the foster care system:

(1) Don't annoy, exasperate, irritate, or in any way bother your foster parents.
(2) Don't fight with the other foster kids in the house. (Sticking to this rule was only possible if you avoided the other kids in the house, so that's what Marin did.)
(3) Never, under any circumstances, tell anyone that you're waiting for your mother to come back for you.

If we rolled Marin's three rules into one, it would say: be invisible. Now, you may think that makes for a lonely sort of life, and you wouldn't be wrong. Marin didn't have any friends, not really. She rarely stayed in one school long enough to make the kind of friend who sticks with you after you go.

She didn't have anyone who loved her. She didn't eat much. She barely spoke above a whisper. If she wanted something, and she couldn't get it for herself, she went without.

But all that was in preparation, you see. When her mother came back for her, she would observe that her daughter hardly took up any space; that keeping Marin would be no trouble at all.

Memory has a way of shifting and dissolving and blending together. When Marin was four, she had hundreds of memories of her mother. They swam beneath her eyelids whenever she closed them: picnics in meadows and sleeping under the stars, circles of drums banging until the sun rose, and the two of them watching the waves roll in and crash against sandstone cliffs.

By the time Marin turned eleven, however, she only had three memories left. The first was of her mother leaning over the blanket where three-year-old Marin lay in a thatch of greenest grass. Her mother's face blocked out the sun, and every stray hair glowed in a golden ring around her head. Marin's pudgy fingers reached up and grasped at the tips of her mother's hair, which hung in curling locks that swung toward the ground.

The second memory was a scolding, from a day when

Marin had slipped a penny through the slot in their piggy bank.

"Why would you want to save something as worthless as money?" Marin's mother shook the piggy bank. The one lone penny clattered around inside, and Marin's mother let loose an exasperated sigh. "This bank is for wishes. Nothing else."

The third memory was of the day Marin's mother left. Marin would have traded that memory for any of the others that had slipped away from her over the years. But that one stuck there in her mind like a skinned knee that you keep bumping into bedposts and banging onto the sidewalk so it never goes away.

G ilda eyed the perilously leaning stack of case files on the corner of her desk and reached for the topmost one. She opened the manila cover and skimmed for pertinent details.

> **Name:** Greene, Marin
> **Age:** 11
> **Age at first placement:** 4
> **Reason for placement:** abandonment
> **Other family:** none
> **Previous placements:** three foster homes and two group homes
> **Comments:** parental release imminent

Eleven is a tricky age in the foster system. Families are eager to adopt an infant with chubby cheeks and pudgy legs and those blinky eyes that haven't seen too much hardship yet. But when a kid turns ten or eleven or twelve, that's when the sad begins to pull at her eyes, when the *I'm not so sure I can trust you* scowl starts to carve lines around her mouth.

Gilda sighed and lifted a stack of papers held together with a paper clip. She peeled back a hot-pink sticky note that read "potential foster-adopt candidates." One by one she turned over the pages, jotting notes in the margins as she read.

The first option was a middle-aged couple whose own children were grown and who discovered they didn't like their empty nest as much as they thought they might.

The second was a family of six who wanted just one more to make it a lucky seven.

And the third was a single woman—a medical doctor, clinical but with a kind disposition. Someone had scribbled a star beside the woman's photo.

Well. We'll see about that.

Gilda shuffled the stack of papers back together until the edges lined up just so, and then she placed the paper clip exactly into the paper clip–shaped indents. She closed the file and tucked it under her arm. She gave her toes one last wide-reaching wiggle and wedged them into her heels.

Gilda was going to have to meet this child herself.

The cost of living in San Francisco is high—skyscraper high. Some people manage by working all-hours jobs. Others rent narrow apartments in old buildings and share with a half dozen friends. Another, less conventional way to make rent is to take in foster kids. Each one comes with an allowance from the state. It can be a job—sort of.

And if you're one of the kids living in a home like that, where you're more of a paycheck than a person, you get to wishing you lived anywhere else. Marin had been in enough foster homes to realize that, bad as this one was, there probably wasn't any better one out there for her. If she ever moved again, it would be because her mother came back for her at last.

Marin stared at her reflection in the cloudy bathroom mirror while she guided her toothbrush in small, jerky circles. Her mother was the only family she had ever known. Marin had always tried not to think about why she left, or worse—why she never returned. But something about being a walking, talking paycheck in this house brought all those questions right up to the surface, like a splinter just deep enough that you can't get it out.

Marin spit, swished a little water around in her mouth, spit again, and walked with whispering footsteps down the hall to the room she shared with three other girls. The door was open, and as she made her way inside, she saw all three girls huddled over something in their hands. It was a book, a small, soft-at-the-edges book. It was *her* book.

There are times when you have to break the rules, even when you're the one who made them.

"Give that back!" Marin cried, and she lunged for her book. But Ashley was ready. She lifted the *I Ching* over her head, where even if the smaller girl took a running leap, she still couldn't reach it.

"What do you want with that old thing, anyway?" That was Becky.

"Musta been her momma's," piped up Amber, the ssss ess sound whistling through the gap between her two front teeth.

Marin grabbed Ashley's arm and tried to yank it

down, but the older girl just laughed and handed the *I Ching* to Becky, who lifted it even higher over her head.

"I bet you can't even read it." Becky opened the book high in the air and squinted at the tiny print. "Preponderance of the—what?" She snapped the book shut.

"I bet she thinks she'll find her Momma momma in there somewhere." Amber again.

Ashley clamped a hand onto her hip. "Her momma's nobody-knows-where. That's what happens when you get left and no one ever comes back for you."

"I heard them talking about it on the phone." By "them,", Becky meant their foster parents. "Her momma doesn't want her, not ever."

Marin stepped on the rail of the lower bunk so she she was nose-to-nose with Becky. "You're a liar!" Marin kicked her in the shin, right in the boniest part, grabbed her pocket-sized *I Ching* while the older girl doubled over, howling, and ran for it.